Scags
at 7

Scags
at 7

Deborah Emin

KEDZIE PRESS
CHICAGO • LONDON

Published by Kedzie Press

Chicago, Illinois

Visit our website at: **www.kedziepress.com**

Cover design and Interior design by Patricia Rasch

Library of Congress Control Number: 2006935135

ISBN-10: 1-934087-33-5
ISBN-13: 978-1-934087-33-6

Printed in Canada
10 9 8 7 6 5 4 3 2 1

For Suzanne who is always so keen-o

Table of Contents

Names

I made up the name that everyone calls me. I made it up because I didn't like the name Mama gave me when I was born when no one could ask me what I wanted to be called. So I'm called, because I say so, Scags. Scags? Mama asked, her voice high and cracking. Scags? Pops said like it was a new penny in his palm. Yes, Scags, I said. That is what I called Pops' cigar when I was two years old and by the time I was four I told them that's what I want to be called. Pops shook my hand, picked me up and twirled me around until I felt like a rope waving straight out from him. I felt dizzy.

Mama said, Your name is Celia. You're named after my mother, Cordelia. Your name is Celia Harper Morgenstern. I can't call you Scags, she said. But Pops said to Mama, Of course you can, she looks like a Scags, red curly top like a lit cigar. She seems so happy when she says call me Scags, how can you refuse?

I was named for my grandmother Cordelia, but she

won't care if I change my name, she's dead. I say that to Mama, She's dead. Mama says, I know, gives me a look like it is a big secret, and then says again, I know, don't remind me. I don't know why Mama wanted to name me after her mother anyway. Mama told me how Cordelia yelled at her all the time and pulled her braids and laid up in bed asking for a glass of orange juice or a cup of tea, not in a nice voice, but in an if-you-please voice. She demanded it and made Mama clean the house and wash the clothes, and always yelling. Mama said Cordelia was only quiet when she was asleep.

Scags is a different sounding name. I listen to my Pops come home and call out Scags and I know who I am. I love the name Scags, SCAAAGS. Scags sounds like a car horn beeping once to say hello, like a leap into dry leaves all raked up in a pile, or like the sound a dog makes, his claws racing on the sidewalk when his owner lets him off the leash.

I think of myself as Scags and that Celia was my baby self, what I was called before I knew what my real name was. Celia's not a special enough name. I don't like the sound of it, like a match flame hitting water, like a bad slip in the sandbox, like a spooky sound coming from the trees at night. It ends. It doesn't begin. When I watch Pops light up his big cigar, take long pulls on it and the tip glows red, redder, orange, it's just like my hair, that's like the tip of me too, all my red hair falling down my back, and I know I need to be called Scags.

I have a feeling about Mama's and Pops' names too. Pops, my Pops, with his wavy black hair, black glasses and cigar had me call him Pops right from the start. When I was little it came out of my mouth so fast that I had to say Pops-Pops. But now I just say one Pops and he smiles at me and he is so tall and handsome and fun that I want to be with him all the time. I said to him, All the kids in this neighborhood call their fathers Daddy. Why are you different? Pops says, he knows that and since he is the only one called Pops that if I'm ever in trouble all I have to do is call out Pops and he'll come running as fast as he can.

Mama?" I ask her, do you like being called Mama? That's what she told me to call her when I was a baby. I like saying Mama, I like whispering Mama when Pops and Mama are talking and how she looks at me, touches my cheek and continues talking to Pops. When I ask her, Do you like being called Mama, she always says, Yes, yes I do, it's what I called my mother.

We live in a brand-new neighborhood. We moved here when I was a baby. There are still empty lots and places to explore. Pops is Jewish and Mama's not. Most of the kids here are Jewish and call their parents Mommy and Daddy. We live here with them and I like the name of the street, Kolmar, and the name of the school, Devonshire, and the name of the place, Skokie, and that there is an Indian village Mama took me to called Maskokie Village where she bought me a bow and arrow. Down the road from there is an amusement park called Ride 'Em where with the tops of milk cartons you can get free rides. I use all my tickets on the roller coaster called Bronco and I sit in the front seat with my best friend Julia whose name I like sometimes and sometimes I get this feeling I'd like to call her what no one else calls her but I don't know what that would be. We sit in the front seat and after the roller coaster climbs to the top of the track, it goes straight down this long, steep hill and I feel the wind against my chest and we yell all the way down because that's what roller coasters are for.

Mama likes to yell too. She'll yell at me and call me Celia when she's angry at me, then she'll yell, Ceeeliaaa, if I've left my bike in the driveway, she yells out of her car to move the bike so she can get into her side of the garage. Or sometimes she yells because I've messed up my room after Odessa cleaned it and made it neat. Mama does like to yell, but she yells mostly at Odessa. Odessa has to keep the house clean as if it were her house and every bit of dirt was her fault. Mama yells at Odessa a lot, that is, until Pops comes home from work. Then she wants to make it nice for Pops. She wants Pops to enjoy the dinner that Odessa cooks up for him, something much better than Mama could ever cook. Mama is a terrible cook.

Odessa has a funny name. I don't know why she has it but it was her Mama's and her great grandmother's name. I like saying it. I like saying O—dess-a as if I was chewing Jujubees, O—chew—dess—chew-a, it tastes so good.

I made up the names for Pops' parents too. I call Pops' pop Boomer because he is so big and booms out when he talks and always says "boom" when I land in his lap. I like calling him Boomer, he's like a baseball caught in a catcher's mitt. And Pops' Mama I call Goldie. She is little, with white, white hair and big ears and wears all this gold jewelry on her ears, around her neck and wrists and has a big gold ring Boomer gave her. It all flashes and shines and she is Goldie.

And if you think those are funny names, how come Boomer and Goldie named Pops' sister Money? Isn't that a funny name? Money honey don't get funny with me. Who's that funny Money's honey?

So we all have our names. I sit on my Pops' lap blowing bubbles with him, only mine always explode on my nose and he sucks his back and breathes out my name, Scags, and it is my name and he is Pops and no one in the neighborhood has names like us.

Last Day At School

I wake up as excited as when I've blown out all the candles on my birthday cake in one blow and know I will get my wish. Today is the last day of school. It is my wish to have a great summer vacation and I will, I know I will, even with Julia going away to camp. I untangle my legs from the sheets, jump right up, pull my nightgown over my head, dress, brush my teeth all so lickety- split and when I look at the mirror over the sink I say, now I am a third grader. Oh.

I go downstairs bringing Odessa my brush so she can fix my hair just right. She is cleaning strawberries, the red of the juice is on her apron and I can tell by how wet her lips are that she has been eating them while she cleans them. Odessa's face is like a soft marshmallow except it is brown instead of white. When she is happy or sad or surprised I can tell by how her eyebrows raise, lower or pucker. And she calls me Funny Face.

She sees me staring at her and she laughs with a

mouthful of strawberries and she calls me that name, Funny Face. I rush to her side and grab onto her, wrap my arms around her, and say, Odessa, do you know what day it is?

She says, Thursday.

No, I say, well yes, I say, but do you know what happens today?

She puts her knife down, rinses her hands. I hand her my brush. She tells me to let go of her so she can fix my long, curly red hair that gets all twisted and knotted in my sleep.

What day is it? Odessa asks.

I whisper, because otherwise I will scream, I say, It's the last day of school.

Ohhh, she says, then you have to look extra special nice to say goodbye to your teacher. Odessa gets the bristles caught in a tangle that hurts as she pulls on it.

Ouch, I say, don't do that.

We've got to little one, you've got a head full of knots. She keeps pulling my head back and I feel like crying.

Pops arrives in the kitchen, whistling When the Saints Go Marching In, tapping his shiny shoes on the shiny floor. Pops is dressed in his green suit, white shirt, green-and-yellow tie. I see he has cut himself shaving.

Be with you in a minute, Mr. Morgenstern, Odessa says, and says to me, What did you do in your sleep last night to make such a mess of this hair? There, she says, and hands me my brush. Finally I think and I go sit at my place at the glass-topped speckled kitchen table. When the sun shines on it, it flashes red, blue, green as if it was pointing to buried treasures, as if Mama or Pops had made a place where magic could happen right in our house.

Pops bends down and kisses me on the cheek. He smells like the purest sunrise and it glows on me. He sits down at the table and Odessa sets his bowl of cereal in front of him. Pops likes Shredded Wheat topped by bananas and strawberries and brown sugar. The bowl sits ready for the milk, which he pours first into his coffee to make it white, then over his cereal.

Pops says, Boomer said if you get a good report card he'll take you to Walker Brothers for an apple pancake. You can go downtown to the office with me.

Oh, keen-o, I say. When? When?

Soon, Pops says, when things slow down a bit. You won't have to wait long. You know Boomer, he loves those apple pancakes as much as you do.

We eat together, making our cereal noises like my Rice Krispies that go snap, crackle, Pops. I finish my glass of milk and go up to Pops and whisper in his ear, I have to go now. Pops taps his fingers on the table.

Where is Mama? he asks, and presto-chango, there she is dressed and ready for the day. It is shopping day when the refrigerator gets packed with food, so much food you'd think there were more people than just us. I love the smell of the fresh ground coffee from the A&P and the onion bread Mama buys for toast on Sunday mornings with our eggs and bacon—Mama's specialty.

I have to go, I say as Mama raises her hand to her black hair, short and curly. I look at her hands. They are so white and soft and she touches her neck, her chest and comes to the table with Pops and me watching her entrance as if she were Queen for the Day. At her place sits half a melon next to a plate of rye toast. She looks at us. She turns to her food and I run down the hall and then I remember I didn't kiss her, I didn't kiss the Mama who is going to be the prettiest Mama at the grocery store. I run back to her and make a lot of noise giving her a big wet one so that she will say, Oh Scags. Out the door I go to pick up Julia.

Julia is waiting on the corner for me. She yells for me to hurry up. I run fast and faster up to her side and tap her on the shoulder and say, You're it. I run, run, run all the way to school which is three blocks away. Julia stays far behind me.

When we get to the playground everyone is lined up ready to go inside. I am out of breath and so hot but it doesn't bother me, I sneak into the line, we march inside to our rooms, and I sit down at my desk in the front row next to Ricky Rappaport. On top of our desks are all the books we studied this year. Our teacher, Mrs. Gillespie, tells the boys to collect the books and for the girls to take the decorations off the bulletin boards and windows.

Mrs. Gillespie looks very nice with her red dress and red scarf around her neck. She doesn't look hot at all. When we finish our work we all sit down and Mrs. Gillespie says, I'm going around the room now to pass out your report cards. You were my best class ever. I really think we studied hard together and you will all remember what we studied this year over the summer, not forget any of it. She smiles, she laughs and so do we. Who could forget Mrs. Gillespie teaching us to tell time with her arms in every direction to show the big and little hands? Who could forget the contest to read and report on the most books and getting all those little stars on our charts for each one?

I am one of the first people she gives their report card to. She bends down, she is very tall. I leave her now, never to see her again and I won't forget her or forgive her for not being my teacher again.

Mrs. Gillespie smiles as she says, Good work, Scags.

I say, This report card better be good because I want to go downtown for apple pancakes. She laughs and sets the card down. I open it. The note says for me to work on my penmanship over the summer and that I'll do really well in third grade along with a whole line of E's, the best I can get.

Ricky Rappaport gets his card next. His crew cut is so new that I can see a big scar on his head from where he got hit by one of the swings that cracked his head open. He stares at his card and holds his head in his hands. I know this is bad news. After seeing my report card, I feel great. After Ricky's it seems unfair, he is not stupid. He just got hurt. I peek at his card and there are lots of U's. His dad is so strict. Ricky, rappy, rickety Rappaport is going to be a rippling, rattling wreck.

He closes his card and looks straight ahead. I flunked, he says, I'm going to have to repeat second grade, I hope I don't get Mrs. Gillespie again. He blinks back his tears.

I don't know what to say, so I say, Want to play Horse after lunch? He shakes his head no.

None of the decorations are left on the bulletin boards. The books have all been picked up and all of a sudden it is dark and quiet.

I think—it's summer— and the bell rings—I have the whole summer to play. We all get up and race for the door yelling, Goodbye, Mrs. Gillespie.

I pick up my report card and run down the hall and I hear Julia yell, Wait Scags, wait for me.

When we get outside, Julia says, I'll let you see my grade card if you let me see yours. Julia stands in the sun.Her long blonde hair looks white. It's all tied up in a ponytail. She is so pretty, so pretty, and she's going to be away most of the summer, gosh. I hand her my card and we start to walk side by side while we look at each other's grades. She got mostly the same grades I did, but I got more E's than her.

Her smile makes me sad. She has her big teeth

11

straight and white while I still have to lose some before I get my big teeth. We walk home. It is hot and quiet. Julia says, Step on a crack, break your mother's back, and then she steps on a crack and laughs. What's wrong, Scags? she asks when I don't laugh.

I say, Now we have the whole summer.

Yeah, she says, and taps me on the shoulder. You're it. She runs and runs and I walk and walk and never step on a crack.

Breath

Pops pops into the kitchen, home from work in the city. He says, Scaags, and then scoops me up, lets my feet touch the ceiling, while my dress falls in my face, and down I come and I set my feet on top of his shoes and we dance that way to his place at the table. Pops sits down and I crawl onto his lap.

I love the smell of his breath—coffee, cigars and the magic of so many words that escaped from between his lips today, each of them leaving their scent in his mouth. Mmm. Yes.

I say, Pops, your breath is mine. I can hold it in my nose for a long, long time. Pops' breath isn't like any other adult's. He doesn't smell old or candied. Mama is always sucking on a mint that does not do anything to get rid of the pack of Marlboros she smokes all day, leaving them burning in the kitchen for Odessa to put out.

To Goldie and Boomer I want to say, I don't like the smell of Listerine. Goldie eats an onion only if

Boomer eats an onion and then she says, All's fair in love and war. Boomer says, The bedroom is the true battleground of humanity. Goldie wrinkles her nose, bites into a scallion and hums.

Pops is always on time for dinner, he likes Odessa's cooking. Mama is straightening the silverware at Pops' place one last time. She bends down and kisses each of us on the cheek. Odessa puts two ice cubes into each water glass, the sound of the ice cracking when she pours the water in makes me think about new pennies. I ask Pops, If I suck on brand new pennies will my breath be bright? Pops laughs at me and says, Bright breaths, as if you could see a breath, as if you would want to.

Pops, I say, I smell your breath everywhere. I can hold it in my nose for a long, long time. I smell his mouth and hold the scent in.

Scags, Pops says as I turn red in the face from holding onto his smell, Scags, he says again and rests his hand on my stomach, there are little hairs in your nose and they hold the smell in, you don't have to choke yourself.

I let out a huge blast of air because I have to tell him he's wrong.

Pops, I say, in science class we learned that the hairs filter and I don't like that because they'll take away the cigar and coffee smells. I know you and you could never not have your cigars and coffee.

Mama says, Come on Scags, get your hands washed,

we're going to eat now.

I scoot off Pops' lap and run to the kitchen sink. Mama says to me in a whisper, It's not polite to stick your face into someone else's. I shrug okay and make my hands all soapy then clap them and watch the bubbles fly.

Odessa says, Funny face, I'd like to go home some-time soon. Odessa has to wait until we finish eating so she can clean up and then Mama takes her to the train station. We eat dinner not too quickly because it is so good, but then before we know it Odessa and Mama are leaving.

Pops and I sit at the now empty table. He has lit up one of his little cigars, a Schimmelpfennig. It smells like burnt gingerbread. If I could catch one of the smoke rings Pops makes and put it in my mouth, it would crunch between my teeth.

Scags, Pops says but he is not looking at me but out the window at the spot by the door where the wind catches.

What is it Pops?

He looks so hard away from me. I need to get up from my chair and go to him. I stick to the seat and it sounds like I'm tearing my skin off when I get up.

I stand next to him. He stares out the window and I try and see what he is looking at but I can't figure it out. Then he says, Metal has no memory.

What do you mean?

He sticks his cigar in his mouth. It has a long ash

that pulses. He puts two hands on the table and grabs the metal frame and says, If you break it, it doesn't know how to fix itself.

I say, You mean it doesn't remember how it used to be?

Pops says, Very good Scags. He lets go of the table and wraps me up in himself. He smells of smoke and coffee, milky coffee the color of wood. He sets his cigar down, holds onto me and stands up, tosses me in the air and with my feet in the air I walk the ceiling until his arms get tired. I settle back down in his lap, my nose on his chin and it is nice this way.

Odessa

First thing when Odessa arrives, she puts up the coffee for Pops and Mama, then calls me down to her. I am all dressed by myself, I'm brushing my teeth. The toothpaste makes me smile. Odessa calls, Little one, are you ready, don't make me climb those stairs yet. I rinse out my mouth, grab my towel for a fast wipe and pick up my hairbrush and the elastics and run down to her. I hear Pops in his bathroom. The shower is pounding him and he is singing, When the Saints Go Marching In.

In the kitchen I find Odessa, in her white dress, white apron and white shoes. Her eyebrows are raised in surprise as she looks through the refrigerator shelves for the strawberries. But she won't find them. Pops and I ate them up last night before I went to bed.

What's the difference between the South Side and the south? I ask Odessa. She stands up and closes the refrigerator, shakes her head from side to side and then laughs at me. I smell her sweat like the air before a storm. Odessa takes my hairbrush out of my hand, and we go where we go every morning, to the table where Odessa sits in Mama's chair to brush my long, long, long red hair that finds a million ways to get tangled, as if little fairies tie it up while I'm sleeping. I once dreamed one of them stood next to my bed and said, Wake up Scags, come to me Scags. I reached out my arm to him and woke up grabbing air.

Odessa says, Why don't you know the difference between the South Side of Chicago and the south of Mississippi, Alabama, and Georgia? I came from the south, Odessa says, from Mississippi and I ended up on the South Side. Odessa comes a long way up to us everyday but Sunday. Her friend Maria drives her up in a big old beat up Ford. Going home though she has to take two trains and a bus because Mama keeps her with us longer than the Rappaports keep Maria.

Stand still, Odessa says, as she yanks, hurts me but when she's done I will have a neat ponytail that keeps me from boiling in this heat. It swings back and forth when I walk. Pops likes to pull on it, yank my head back, and give me a kiss on the tip of my nose.

Pops comes into the kitchen just when Odessa finishes with my hair. Pops looks at me and says, How's my sweet patutti fruity?

Odessa says, I've got your coffee ready but someone ate up all those strawberries I cleaned yesterday.

Pops says to Odessa, I confess.

Me too, I say.

Pops goes to his spot at the table and sits down. He says to me, That razzmatazz smile going to get you a whole lot of jazz. Odessa and I both laugh. Pops says, Don't laugh, I'm waking up my vocal chords. I've got to be excited and smart, a fast talker and a man on time to make those customers sit up and listen.

Pops wears his brown suit, brown loafers, and brown socks. He slowly eats his cereal without strawberries. He looks so handsome with his hair slicked back, his black glasses sitting on his nose. His fingers on his left hand are beating out a tune but I don't know what it is. I say, What's that you're tapping out?

Before Pops finishes what's in his mouth, Odessa sings out all the words as if she were climbing that stairway to paradise. You could see her making her way to the top of it as she moved from my chair to Pops'.

Pops puts down his spoon and claps and says, Very good Odessa. Excellent singing. Crisp articulation. Don't you think Odessa sang that well? Pops asks, Don't you think Odessa has a great set of pipes? He taps me on the shoulder. I look at him sitting with the sun in his glasses and a smile on his face.

Pops asks, Don't you feel chipper this a.m.?

What's an a.m.? I ask.

He says, Ante midi, a.m., before noon, and p.m. is post midi, after noon. See Scags you can learn in and out of school.

Yeah, I say, not wanting to do anything but play. Can I go out now? Pops says, Do what you do, do what

19

you do. He jumps up from the table, standing he drinks his light, light coffee. Sets the cup down and leaves. He is gone. It is so quiet. I have the whole day to play and tonight is Friday night, the night Odessa stays with me all night while Mama and Pops go out with their friends. Odessa and I and maybe Julia, will listen to Louis Armstrong records and Ella Fitzgerald, all cozy in my room.

There are two beds but I listen to the music snug up tight on my bed with Odessa. She is so soft, filled up with the music and humming under her breath. I feel the vibrations in her chest. Sometimes she says, I could have done that, when Ella sings low. I love this music coming out of Odessa. So does Julia who gets up and dances, her blonde ponytail swinging back and forth. We can all lie on my bed, the three of us. When Julia goes home, Odessa helps me get ready for bed. She gets into the other bed and hums Billie Holiday songs, but they seem so sad I have to fall asleep.

At the Beach with Mama
And Aunt Money

Pops has to work this Saturday afternoon, so Mama and I are going to meet Aunt Money at Ardmore Beach. Mama is in her bedroom, naked. I like to see Mama without her clothes on. First thing that comes into my mind is I'm going to look like her when I grow up. Mama doesn't like me to stare at her, so the second thing I think is, look fast. Mama has a long skinny body, dark skin and a big belly button. Her tushy is kind of big, too. When I look at her I think I would like to swim into her arms and rest my cheek on her shoulder and stay like that for a million years. Keen-o.

Scags, Mama says, because she caught me staring at her, put on your suit and sandals, I'll get everything else. She bends down to pull up her suit. I run to my room, past the jar of snails and try to remember where Odessa put my new white suit with the flowers on it. Mama, I call, I don't know where my suit is. Mama comes into my room and naturally it is in the first

21

place she looks.

When we get to the beach, I walk with all my toys to the spot we usually go to. There is Aunt Money with an umbrella up and a couple of seats and a big white towel over her so that she gets no sun on her at all. It's kind of chilly right now. The umbrella swings and whips in the wind. Not too many people are here yet. I know the water is going to be cold and I think, look at those big waves crashing so hard they could break the ground.

I bend over Aunt Money and give her a big wet one. She goes, Scaaags, and we both giggle. She has her hair tied up under a white hat and even here at the beach she looks pretty and smells good. I drop all my toys at her feet. She wiggles her red toe nails. Mama says, Let me put some lotion on you, because your skin is even whiter than Aunt Money's. I sit down next to Mama. She squeezes out some white stuff and rubs me all over. I love the coldness on my shoulders and get goose bumps.

I jump up, grab my bucket and run to the shore where Lake Michigan makes such a noise. A lifeguard with a big gob of white goop on his nose and the reddest shoulders I've ever seen comes over to me and says, You can't go in today. I ask, Why not? He says something about an undertoad and sometimes that happens in Lake Michigan. Giant frogs love the bottom of the lake, Pops has told me, and you have to be very careful. I run back to Mama and say, I can't go swimming today, there is an undertoad. Aunt Money laughs and says, Undertow not undertoad. I ask, What does that mean? Aunt Money takes my hand and pulls me down onto her lap.

An undertow, she says, is when there is a strong current at the bottom of the water that sucks everything and everyone to the center of the lake and you can drown. Really? I say. How does that happen? Aunt Money pushes the tip of my nose and says, It has something to do with wind, moon, tides. I'm no scientist. I jump off her lap and say, Wind, moon, tides. An undertow. I'll have to ask Pops about this. He'll know.

I can tell that Mama and Aunt Money have been talking about things they think I don't understand, because Mama has her Scags-should-be-seen-not-heard look on. So I say, Aunt Money do you have a boyfriend?

Aunt Money lets out one of her big howls that sounds high then low like a hiccough turning into a burp. Scags, Aunt Money asks, what kind of woman would I be if I didn't have a boyfriend?

Mama says, Scags, how about sitting here without asking all your questions? I sit down between Mama and Aunt Money and show Mama I am zipping my lips.

Mama says, Money, I thought you got rid of that man.

Aunt Money says, I had to take him back. It broke my heart to see how easily he could get along without me. Mama and Aunt Money laugh but I don't see what's so funny.

Money turns to Mama and says, Let's bury Scags. I ask, What for? Aunt Money says, Just from the waist down. Come on, it'll be fun. Aunt Money pulls her towel back and begins to dig at the sand with my green shovel. I say, I really don't like this game. Mama says, Don't worry, we won't leave you. She takes my bucket and scoops piles and piles of sand away. Aunt Money leans over the hole and I can see her breasts. They are bigger than Mama's and as white as snow. I want to fall into them as if they were drifts, as if the world was one big snowbank and I could fall into it and not be cold.

Aunt Money says, Come sit here, pointing to the big hole. It's not very deep but wet, a little like getting into the bathtub. I slip into the spot and they cover me with lots of sand. My arms are free. When I wiggle my toes the sand cracks so Mama pats it down again. I sit still. Mama and Aunt Money sit back and turn to each other.

Mama says, You know Money, no one in your family likes you to be with this colored man.

I turn my head to look at Aunt Money. She has a sly smile on her face. I know that smile. Pops has that smile. I say, You smile just like Pops when he has a secret.

Oh yeah, Aunt Money says, and turns to Mama and says, Smart kid.

Mama says, Sometimes too smart. Look Money, I just want you to be happy and if this colored man—

Aunt Money says, Burdette, Burdette Williams.

I ask, What kind of name is Burdette?

Mama says, Scags, remember what I said about keeping quiet? I nod yes and wonder why doesn't Mama let me talk, I'm here too. I lean my head back and close my eyes. I wander back and forth between being at the top of the waves and then skip around in my head to Mama's and Aunt Money's voices. I hear the hard fist of the lake on the sand. I don't care that Aunt Money has a colored boyfriend. Mama tells her that she can't bring him over, because what would the neighbors think and then I really am asleep. Big blue waves cut big chunks out of a big blue sky and throw them hard and harder until I have to run from the undertoads in my overshoes. I'm spinning and spinning. Their voices are so soft and cool, back and forth with the waves knocking them over. I see writing in the sand—MAN, COLORED MAN—and hear Odessa sing, Oh my man I love him so but he'll never know—and what is Odessa doing here? I wake up. The two of them are gone—oh my—I pull and push out of the sand. Once I'm out of that hole I turn to the Lake. There they are. I run to the water and push myself between them. They are like sisters. Mama takes one hand, Aunt Money the other. They swing me back and forth over the white foam on the waves and I say keen-o and want to give each of them a big wet one.

6

Julia Says

Summer is hot, it is always hot. Sometimes the day is so hot that the sky turns white as if the sun has melted all the clouds. Bright. It hurts my eyes. Julia and I are in her bedroom where Julia is strumming on her guitar and I am beating out the beat on the bongos. I think summer is for having fun. Julia is sort of playing the guitar, her mother taught her some songs, and on her face is her look. I know that look, that I-don't-want-to-have-to-do-anything look.

Lying in the sun, I think, would be okay if Julia wants to use her slip and slide to cool off on. I say, How about that slip and slide? Julia gets a big-eyed grin on her face, so that where at first she seemed so lazy, now she seems full of beans. She jumps off her bed, opens her bottom dresser drawer, pulls out one of her old, too small bathing suits to give to me, a navy blue one with big white buttons to hold the straps up. She takes out a new one for herself, pink and orange, that shows off her tan.

We quickly pull off our clothes even our shoes and socks and leave them in a pile at the foot of each bed in Julia's room. Julia goes to the linen closet in the hallway and pulls out two towels. She hands me a big brown one that smells so fresh like the sun soaked it through and through and is so soft like the fur on Mama's winter coat. We're going to lie on them on Julia's patio.

We run outside, yelling Yah, Yah, Yah, past Mrs. Arthur, who has red hair and freckles just like me. She asks, what's going on? Julia tells her and she says, Scags, I'll be right out with some lotion for you. Sit under the umbrella, she says.

We race out the back door, down the walk to the patio. The cement is so hot on the bottoms of my feet that I run fast on my toes like a ballet dancer getting quickly across the floor. I jump onto the nearest chair.

The patio is a square on the side of the Arthurs' house. Around it are a couple of oak trees with a garden separating it from the grass. Its floor is covered with big rectangular slabs of green and pink stones. Grass grows between them, around them, through them like the hair in Mr. Arthur's ears. Julia gets the hose and sprays her feet. Now that I am settled on the lawn chair, my feet barely remember the heat.

Get under the umbrella, Julia says, you don't want to burn up and get sick. I think, yes I do, I'll get so sick that Julia can't go away, that she'll have to sit in my room, holding my hand as I go closer and closer to death. I pull my chair under the umbrella. I'm too young to die.

The light is so white and it hasn't rained in days. The snap dragons, roses, and geraniums wait for the rain, all drooping a bit with the weight of the heat, the curse of heat as Odessa says. This a-cursed heat, she says and wipes her face with her apron. The heat is with us because it's summer time, I think, and if it wasn't such a great time to be hot, to sweat and stink and need a bath every night before going to bed, if the grass wasn't green and the sky blue and the earth black, what fun would it be?

Mrs. Arthur comes outside wearing her yellow halter top and green short shorts. She's carrying a big pitcher of iced tea, a tube of suntan lotion and a magazine. Her skin looks as white as mine. She lies down under the umbrella too while Julia pulls out the slip and slide. I close my eyes and the colors are so bright and move so fast behind my eyelids that I open my eyes very fast and even with them open I see the pinpoints of red, orange, purple, yellow float in the air. Mrs. Arthur sits up, squeezes the lotion out of the tube onto my back and arms, legs, chest, face. It feels so nice to have her touch me, the lotion is cold, her fingers are strong and can wrap themselves around my arms. You are like a bird, she says, all fine and fragile. When she's done, I lie back down. The smell of lotion mixes with the scent of the heat and flowers.

28

It smells like I could eat it but I'm sure the smell is better than the taste.

Julia says, Come on Scags, do it, slip and slide yourself. The red plastic slide lays flat on the grass. Julia has the hose on it, turned on hard, and when you fall on it, you slide all the way to the end of it. I jump up out of the chair, dance over the floor, jump over the little garden and run and run, race my legs harder and harder until I fly over the ground until my legs can't run any harder. Then out I go like a diver off a board, I sail up and then down on my belly, so hard, so hard that the wind is knocked out of me. I twist and shake all the way down the red plastic slide, the water in my eyes, mouth, even ears. I try hard to get my breath back but I'm giggling too hard to breathe right.

Julia is standing at the end. Her hair is all in little clumps. She's got her hands over her mouth as she jumps from one leg to the other. You goose, she says, you have to bend over to land on your stomach, not jump up. She laughs and laughs and I sit on the grass, catching my breath. I say, Oh yeah, I forgot.

We run and slide, run and slide. The water goes up my nose sometimes and into my eyes. Mrs. Arthur finally gets up and goes inside. Now we have the patio all to ourselves. Julia turns off the water and we splash the puddles on the slide at each other. Let's have some tea, I say, and give Julia one last splash with my feet and then run to the patio.

The sun has moved in the sky. The patio is almost

all in shade from the trees around us. I pour Julia a glass of tea. She says something surprising to me, My mother is going to have a baby. A baby? I ask. Julia says, I'm going to get to babysit in a couple of years and to hold the baby's bottle and have a brother or sister to play with. I say, Will you still be my friend? Julia looks up from her glass of iced tea, smiles. Julia says, Of course we'll be friends, we'll always be friends.

I don't have a baby sister or brother. I don't know what that will be like for Julia.

I have to pee, Julia says.

All of a sudden I feel like going home. I follow Julia into her house, watching her butt twist back and forth as she walks. I get my clothes out of her room and carry them all bunched up against my wet stomach. Mrs. Arthur watches me from the kitchen. Ready to go home, Scags? she asks and I tell her yes and thank her for the iced tea. I walk out their front door, around the corner and up the driveway of my house. A baby, I think. Mama could have a baby, too. Maybe she doesn't want anyone else but Pops and me. But she could try.

Pops and Scags Go Downtown

Pops holds my hand as we go into his office downtown in the Palmolive Building. The glass in the outer door has Boomer's name first and big and Pops' name second and smaller. I stick my hand through the mail slot and wave inside saying, We're here Boomer, hi Boomer. Pops tells me to be quiet, that Boomer may be on the phone. When we get inside, Pops lets go of my hand and I run into Boomer's big corner office. His desk is huge and has a long table facing him so he could have big meetings with big people and I love sitting on Boomer's desk.

Boomer is on the phone. When we walk in he looks at his watch. He places a hand over the phone's mouth and says to Pops, Annie can't make it today. Sit out front until Goldie gets here. Pops shrugs his shoulders and says to me, Come along, and we go into his office which is much smaller than Boomer's. The desk is smaller but brighter than Boomer's. I sit down behind it. It is so neat. Not like my desk at home. I am a slob. I sit down in Pops' big chair and run my hands over the green blotter. It feels cool and soft like it would be keen-o to write or color on. What do you know, Pops opens his briefcase and there is my super large coloring book, my big box of crayons and my checkers set. I say, Pops, did you bring this for me? He smiles and empties the rest of his big black briefcase. Out come all these different colored pieces of paper, stacks of them. He places them on a corner of the desk and says, I'm going to leave you in here for a while until Goldie comes. I'll just be in front. He takes off his jacket, pulls at his white shirt, hangs the jacket in a little closet, and takes his handkerchief out of his back pocket and wipes the skin between his nose and lips.

Pops, I ask, can I play office too? What I like to do is have his old colored pieces of paper and write on them even though they are already filled with words I don't understand. Pops says, Sure, and reaches around the desk, opens his big bottom drawer and pulls out a stack of paper. Yes. This is going to be fun. He puts the papers in front of me and takes his pen out of his shirt pocket and gives it to me. We can hear Boomer's voice but not what he is saying. He laughs a lot. Boomer booms.

Pops leaves me and goes to the secretary's desk. I pretend that I am in charge here. I'm the boss. I click Pops' pen and the little tip peeks out. On the top sheet of paper I write, Scags says to write to a man and tell him we want to make a lot of money. Boomer slams the phone down and then yells something at Pops. They talk in loud voices while I do all the work.

I make checks and x's on every one of the sheets Pops gave me. I work very hard, very hard because I like making the stack smaller and smaller. The pink, green, and yellow paper is so thin and the writing on it is so blurry, I wonder how Pops can read it. When I finish, I pick up my checkers and go into Boomer's office. It is so bright and cool in here. Boomer is reading the newspaper, looks over the top and winks at me.

Boomer says, I see you have your checker set. Want to try and beat an old pro? Yeah, I say and walk over to him. Boomer picks me up and sets me boom down on his big desk that has all these keen-o things on it. There are brass pieces of engine machinery that are so heavy. Every time I go to pick one up, I can't do it with one hand. They are so strange looking, like birds in some way, on one foot bending over each other, trying to get a cool drink of water.

Boomer folds up his newspaper, takes the checkers from me and sets it up. I tell Boomer, I like being red. He switches the board and says, What makes a winner? I answer, Having the first move. Presto-chango before I can believe it, I had the first move and he beat me. Whoa Boomer, I say, how did you beat me? I had the first move. Boomer says, We'll try again. I do. I move one of the ones in the center and yes I do win. Boomer asks me, Are you getting hungry for that hot and sweet apple pancake?

I hear Pops talking to Goldie. Why is Goldie here? I ask Boomer. He picks me up off the desk and sets me back down on the floor. I smooth my dress. Goldie comes into Boomer's office. She is really golden today in her sleeveless gold dress and gold shoes. I say, Hi Goldie. She says, Don't I get a kiss? I run over to her and give her a big wet one on the cheek. I feel her hand behind my ear and then when I pull away a nickel is in her palm. She smiles a big smile as if she just did the keenest thing in the world, the whole world. I say to her as I take the nickel, I'm the boss here. Dropping my voice down low I ask Goldie, Don't you think it's time to eat? Goldie presses her lips to my cheek and I know she left her lipstick mark there. I rub my cheek. Goldie licks her finger and erases the smudge from my face.

Pops, I say, oh Pops. Pops is on the phone. Boomer looks at his watch and says, Well if we're going to eat, let's go. Pops, I say again but Boomer takes my left hand and Goldie takes my right hand and while Pops sweats at the secretary's desk, his handkerchief wiping the back of his neck, he doesn't see us leave. Why can't he come too? I ask Boomer. But we walk out the door, down the hall, into the elevator, across the lobby to the street. Everybody knows Boomer. He likes to say, This is my granddaughter. Everybody looks down at me. I try to smile like Mama says to do but Pops got left behind. Pops is doing all the work.

Bookmobile I

On Thursdays the bookmobile pulls up at the corner in front of Julia's house. It is tan and brown with two doors and two sets of wooden steps, one for us to go in and one for us to go out. The bookmobile lady is very old and always has ink stains on her green blouse and on the tips of her fingers. She sucks on her pens and wears a scarf covering up all her hair which I bet is pure white. She doesn't talk to me, she likes to read and she doesn't like us to talk. Us is me and Julia.

I see a book on the top shelf with an orange and green colored cover with black letters that say SCIENCE IN YOUR OWN BACK YARD. I reach and reach and stretch so hard my blouse pulls out of my shorts and I feel a little breeze from the fan the bookmobile lady has turned on. She won't get up to help me, I'm sure, but I ask anyway.

Excuse me please, but I can't reach. Up she jumps, tall with bermuda shorts on and white knee high socks and a pair of old cracked loafers. Which one, she asks

me. I tell her and she pulls it down. Before handing it
to me, she looks through it, turns the pages fast and
says, good choice. She hands me the book.

It smells new and I check my pocket to make sure
I have my library card, because I definitely want this
book. I open it to the first page. It says, lie down on
your stomach for ten minutes and then on your back
on the grass in your back yard and see what you can
discover of the natural world.

The natural world, I say out loud. Julia, on the step
stool above me says shush. I show her the book. She
bounces a little, shakes her head and smiles down at
me. Jumping off the stool quietly, she shows me the
book she's looking at of kings and queens. Her new
idea is that kings and queens have all the fun because
they get to dress up all the time. I should have been a
princess, she whispers in my ear. Yes, I say and don't
know what else to say.

I pull out my library card and go up to the bookmobile lady and tell her I want this book. She asks me is
that all I want, she's not going to be back for another
week. I say in a whisper, I've got a lot to do this week.
She asks, What are you going to do? I say, It's Julia's
last week before she goes away to camp and we're
going to have fun. The lady nods and I put the card
and book on her little desk. She opens the cover, pulls
out the borrower's sheet, stamps it and puts a card in
the pocket with next Thursday's date.

I go down the going out steps and tell Julia, Let's go.

She is still busy looking at pictures of kings and queens. I'll see her later. I run to my back yard. I open the book to that first page and lie on my back and read.

It tells me to close my eyes, be still and listen, smell, feel. I listen. I smell. I feel. There is the sound of the cicadas in the cottonwood tree and a lawn mower a ways away. There's Mama's voice yelling at Odessa about the dust she found on the sills in the living room. I smell the heat. It's a perfume, sweet like the roses but nasty too. The ground is a hard bed for me to lie on and I'm shaded by this big old tree.

Scags, Scags, Mama calls. With all the windows open I hear her but she doesn't see me lying on this green blanket with my legs crossed at the ankles, anyone's lazy girl right now. She yells at Odessa that I'm nowhere to be found. She's leaving now to run her errands and she'll go without me. I don't hear what Odessa says.

I turn over and look very closely at the ground. The grass is very green and spotted with bugs. Under the grass is very black ground and when I put my face in it, the blades of grass go up my nose and tickle. I see the white puffs of fluff from the cottonwood like powdered sugar. I lie on my back and stare at the sky through the branches. I fall through the blue holes between the clouds. I clutch my book to my chest.

From her yard, Julia calls me but I'm too happy here under my tree to move. Scags. Scags. She keeps saying my name but I pretend I am asleep while my name bounces off the trees and bushes, off the house, off the ground. Julia stops calling me. Silence. All the noise is gone. I could fall into the quiet but then Julia is lying next to me. She taps my shoulder. She whispers, Scags, I'm here. I put my finger to my lips. She says, Okay. The two of us lie still as two caterpillars in the same cocoon, waiting.

The Tickling Game

In my room, where the dresser drawers have just been cleaned out by Odessa and the closet put in order and the desk dusted and my chair dusted and the record player closed for a rest, the tickling game is on my mind. Julia is coming up the stairs to my room, wearing her mother's black velvet evening cape with the red lining. I'm messing up my bed that Odessa just fixed and boy would I love to jump from bed to bed, but Mama would be angry.

Julia comes in my room, jumps next to me and tickles my arm. When I don't laugh, she tickles my neck. Now if I don't laugh, she'll tickle my stomach and if I still don't laugh, I win, unless I do all of that to her and she doesn't laugh. Julia's so ticklish that sometimes just saying—want to play the tickling game?—she giggles.

It is hot and giggling makes me hotter. Julia's leaving tomorrow in the heat, in the early morning before I get up. Mr. and Mrs. Arthur are going to take her to the train station and for the very first time, Julia will be away for more than just a day or two. I tickle Julia a little harder and she jumps on top of me, tickles my stomach and no matter how much I say no fair, no fair, she doesn't stop or can't stop or won't stop and I almost wet my pants.

Pops opens his bedroom door across the hall and comes to my room. He has a look on his face like he swallowed something funny, but he looks as if he doesn't know us. I jump off the bed and walk over to him and take his hand.

Pops, I say real low, Pops, are you okay? He nods and lets go of my hand and goes back to his room and before he closes his door, he tells me to close mine. As soon as my door is closed, Julia takes the cape and hides under it and we start to giggle and giggle and the funniest thing is I don't know what's so funny.

The door swings open just as I jump onto the other bed in my room and pull out the clean pillow. It's Pops again. He's got his hands in fists at his sides and he looks like he is going to yell. He says, Just what the hell is all of this noise about? I sit down on the bed. Julia comes and sits next to me, wrapping her cape around her.

I hear Mama coming up the stairs and she asks Pops what he is angry about, she says, Nate, they're little girls. Let them be little girls somewhere else, he says, and walks back to his room and slams the door.

Mama looks at what we have done to the beds

and comes into my room and straightens out the bed-spreads and pillows, shooing Julia and me out of the room. She says, Go play somewhere else for a while, Pops needs to take a nap, he's tired.

We run quietly but quickly out of my house and go to Julia's where it is dark and cool. All the shades are drawn. We sneak into the kitchen looking for some treats to take to Julia's bedroom. Sitting on the kitchen table is her mother's purse, her big black leather one with the broken strap and zipper. It's the bag she carries everywhere. We look inside it and there in the pocket is a brown cigarette case and matches. Julia looks at me and I shrug my shoulders. She opens the cigarette case slowly in case Mrs. Arthur is watching us, she then quickly pulls out two cigarettes and hands me one and takes the matches. I've never lit a match before, I say, and Julia looks at me as if I am retarded.

Let's go to the bathroom, she says, and when we get inside she turns the fan on. The whirring noise covers my giggles. What are you laughing at? Julia wants to know. She pulls a match out of the book and strikes it on the black piece, it flashes into flame and she holds it up to my face. I blow it out because I can't stop laughing. Julia stamps her foot. She tells me to be serious and I can see she is getting angry at me, so I hold the cigarette up to my lips. Julia lights it with another match and holds it to the tip. I take a breath like I've seen Mama do and the smoke is hot

41

and minty and burns my throat. The smoke goes up
my nose and my head is dizzy. Julia lights her own
cigarette and swallows it all down she starts coughing
so loud that I throw my cigarette and hers into the
toilet and listen to the hiss of the flame in water. I'm
afraid her mother will discover us. I flush the toilet
but they don't go down. I flush again and again and
finally they disappear. I feel sick to my stomach, I say,
I want to lie down.

Julia says, Go to my room and I'll put the matches
back. I lie on her bed, staring at her ceiling waiting
for her to return. Well this is it, I say, as she goes
to the other bed and lies down. You leave tomorrow
morning.

I leave you my evening cape, Julia says to me, and
unties it and throws it to me. I catch it by its torn edge
where Julia has pulled and pulled at it. It smells like
cigarettes and dust. Thanks, I say, but I don't want it.
I throw it back to her. She sits up and catches it and
looks at me and asks, Why not? I know I've got to be
honest because she is going away for a long time and
I'll feel bad if I tell her a lie now.

I don't like it, I say, it looks old and ratty. There
I said it and the cape is Julia's favorite thing of her
mother's. Although, I know that that big diamond
ring her father, who is really not her father, her real
father she never knew, anyway Mr. Arthur gave Mrs.
Arthur the ring that Julia told her mother she wants
when she dies is really her favorite thing.

I say to Julia, You're going to be gone for a long time.

All summer, she says.

I say, Are you scared?

Julia laughs and says, Why should I, why should I get scared at going away when it's going to be so much fun with horseback riding, swimming, waterskiing and a cabin full of girls?

But you don't know any of them, I say.

That's true, she says, but maybe they'll all be nice and fun. I've never left home alone, she says. Oh well, she sighs, it'll be fun and before you know it I'll be back. That's what my mother says.

I hope so, I say, and I ask myself if Mrs. Arthur is going to be as sad as me that Julia's gone?

Now That Julia Is Gone

It's not so usual to have a day without Julia. But it's going to get usualer and usualer. I leave my house with my Davy Crockett hat on and wear my holster and gun that Pops says I can't play with in the house. I have caps in the pistol that I bought the other day and haven't used yet. I like the little boxes they come in and opening the gun and threading them in almost more than shooting them. I want to take a ride on my bike with the training wheels still on. I push it out of the garage, take a fast ride down the drive and a sharp right onto the sidewalk, the bike riding on only one of the training wheels.

There is all this time all this time and no Julia. No going for rides with her around the block. No sitting in her bedroom playing bongos. We won't play the tickling game for a long time. Although the sun is out, the air is very wet and you can see it wrapped in the branches of the trees. I turn the corner past Julia's house. The front door is closed and the garage door is closed. Then I go past the new house, the house they just finished building and there's a boy standing on the corner. He's got a holster and gun, and a bandanna around his neck. I ride right past him and he calls after me, Hey can't you stop a minute?

Of course I can, so I get off my bike and turn it around and then get back on it. He says, What's the matter, you chicken, can't you ride without them training wheels? My cheeks get hot and my throat tightens. I say, I never tried. He says, What's the matter with you, you're too old to be riding around like that. Want me to take them off? My name's Davy, he says. I say, Hi, my name is Scags. What kind of name is that? Davy asks. It's my name, my own name, that no one else has. I like it, Davy says.

He pulls the gun out of his holster and shoots three shots in the air. I feel silly pulling my gun out, but I do and aim the shots at him. Bam, bam, bam. You're dead, I say. He grabs his shirt and makes a face and falls to the ground. He doesn't mind dying I see, but I do. I hate it when someone says to me, bang you're dead. I like to run and fight. I like being on my own horse racing around, ride up to a fort and kill all the Indians in there and run away screaming and yelling that I've won.

Davy stands up. He says, Want me to take those baby wheels off? I see no reason not to. He leads me to the garage where a big red Cadillac sits and he pulls out a big green and rusty tool box. He opens it and says, This was my dad's. He was an auto mechanic. What happened to him? I ask. Davy says, He died in a car crash. He left us lots of money. Wow, I say, so you just live with your mother in this big house? Just the two of you? He nods his head yes while he pulls out a wrench and then loosens the nuts on the training wheels and off they come one, two, three. I've been holding the bike while Davy works. I put the kickstand down and look at my bike with its dull blue color and big tires and white seat. Davy puts the tool box away, takes the training wheels and hands them to me. Then he gets on the bike and rides off. Hey, I say, drop the training wheels and go after him. He isn't riding fast so when I catch up with him, I yank his shirt and pull him over.

He says, What you doing, I'm just showing you how to ride. I say, I know how to ride, now get off. He gets off saying he could have gone faster if it had been a boy's bike. I get on the bike and start riding, and ride and ride, it is so simple. My face feels like it's being scrubbed and scraped by the wind. My knuckles hurt from how hard I am grabbing the handlebars. I wonder if I'll be able to turn the corner, so I slow down a bit, the bike wiggles. I turn and go down to the bottom of the hill and put my brakes on and get off the seat to turn the corner. Back on the bike, I fly down the rest of the block, past the Mills sisters' house and the empty lot and the Cooks'. I'm riding so fast that tears fly from my eyes and my legs get tired.

Won't Julia be surprised when she comes home and I'm riding my bike without training wheels? I stop in front of my house and lie down on the front stoop, my bike at my side, my gun in its holster and this new kid coming around the corner looking for me.

11

Morning Talk

Pops is in bed today. Mama tells Odessa to be quiet when she cleans upstairs. She takes her hot coffee and her lawn chair and goes to the front stoop to have her usual morning talk with Mrs. Arthur. I come too and put my arms around Mama's shoulders and whisper in her ear, What's wrong with Pops? She sips her coffee. It is hot and so black that I see steam rising around her eyes. Mama is dressed for the day. Mama wants to talk to Mrs. Arthur, who appears from her house and sets a chair down and the two of them raise their coffee cups and say good morning. I try and get onto Mama's lap but she pushes me away. Can't you see I'm dressed up? Mama asks. Yes, Mama is dressed for the day in a sleeveless white blouse and a navy pleated skirt, her white sandals show off her red toe nails.

Mrs. Arthur asks, How's Nate? Now I say out loud, What's wrong with Pops that he's staying in bed today? Mama yanks on my hair and I know I have said something I'm not supposed to say. Mama yanks my head back. I see blue sky and smell her perfume. Mama says very quietly, Scags if you insist on being here you have to be quiet. Nothing's wrong with Pops, he's a little under the weather. I look again at the blue sky and wonder what weather he is under but I know I can't ask Mama now.

Mama says, How are you feeling Ginger? You're not showing much yet. Showing what? I ask. Mama gives me one of her don't-push-me looks and I let go of her and sit on the stoop, my back to her and listen. I like to listen. I like the sounds of Mrs. Arthur's and Mama's voices going back and forth like a nice game of badmitton.

The stoop is hard and hot already. Mama is sitting in the sun, but Mrs. Arthur is in the shade. Mrs. Arthur says, You know Beverly there is something to this pregnancy that is very gratifying. Maybe because Mort waited so long to have a family that he is more attentive and concerned than Julia's father was.

What does attentive mean? Who was Julia's father? Julia never talks about him. Julia's at camp. She's probably on a horse right now, going for a long ride on top of a big brown, no black, horse. She probably thought up a name to call him that no one knows except her and the horse. I wish she would write to me or come home already.

Mama says, Nate and I weren't married very long when I got pregnant with Scags. Mrs. Arthur says,

And you weren't with anyone— Oh no, Mama says very fast and the two of them giggle like Julia and me do when the tickling game starts. So what do they mean and what are they talking about? I stamp on some ants circling around my shoes and get up and do a little soft shoe, as Pops calls it, and squinch the ants, make them disappear.

Mrs. Arthur says, I am still sick at night, I go to Julia's room to toss and turn and not disturb Mort. He needs eight hours when he has to work.

Mr. Arthur owns a button factory. He took Julia and me there once and it wasn't very big or interesting except for how he held each of us by the hand and introduced us to everyone as his newest girlfriends. He gave me a bag of buttons, all kinds of buttons and when I came home, Aunt Money was there and showed me how to sew them onto a piece of cloth. It was wintertime and we made a snowman filled with button eyes, nose, mouth and then put a row of buttons down his chest as if he wore a coat. Julia threw her buttons away.

Mama says, When I told Nate I was pregnant, he couldn't keep his hands off me. But when I got big, and boy did I get big, I started to waddle and that drove him nuts. One minute he was yelling at me, the next minute, as I sat there crying, he apologized. I wondered who was having the baby.

I say softly, Pops and Mama were having me together.

Mrs. Arthur asks, Are you going to have another child?

I can hear in Mama's voice a far away sound as if Mrs. Arthur and I weren't here. As if she was talking in my dream. Mama says, We talk about it, we talk, and talk, but I don't know. The energy it takes to chase after, changing diapers, feeding, sleeping . . .

She says these words so that I see pictures in my head. I see a little baby in a crib. It is dark out. There is a thunderstorm. The room gets white lighted and Mama is holding my hand. I start to cry and Mama goes, shush, shush.

Mama says, Nate became ultrasensitive to noise what with all the noises Scags made. I guess we'll just be three. That's enough for me.

For me too, I guess.

I ask Mama, Was I a noisy baby?

Mama laughs and comes back to us. Yes, she says, you were always making some sound or another. But normal sounds, and it wasn't so bad. Pops is just a little tempermental.

Oh, I say, and stand up and put my arm around Mama's shoulder and she raises her hand and touches my cheek. Mama says, Don't you think you've got a pretty good deal here? She laughs out loud. She raises her cup to her lips but it is empty.

Mrs. Arthur says, I like the age these fine girls are at.

Mama asks, How's Julia at camp? Yeah, I say, she

hasn't written to me yet. Mrs. Arthur says, Don't hold your breath for a letter from that child. We have to call her to hear anything. Julia is having fun horseback riding and swimming but she hates the food.

We should send her some of Odessa's cookies, I say to Mama.

She'd like that, Mrs. Arthur says, but you know she'll be back here lickety-split. Do you miss her Scags?

I say, Yes, I do, Julia's my best friend.

Mama stands up, picks up her chair and says to Mrs. Arthur, Nice chatting with you Ginger. Why don't we go to that new restaurant on Green Bay Road today or tomorrow, that is if you're up to it.

Mrs. Arthur doesn't stand up. She stays in her spot on the stoop of her back door. Beverly, she says, you are a woman after my own heart. But what about Nate? Can you leave him?

Mama says, He'll be fine, just needs to sleep. Right Scags?

I say, Yes, he's just tired. Just tired.

They agree to meet at 1:00 and they are best friends like Julia and me and I jump off the stoop, land plop on my feet and run to the garage and get my bike and go looking for Davy. Everything is keen-o today.

Davy's Mother

I get on my bike and ride around the corner to see if Davy is home. He's not in his yard, so I put my bike down and go up the big front stairs and ring the doorbell which sounds like a big gong gone off. I am afraid of how loud it is. I hear someone walking in the house with heavy footsteps. The door opens a crack and there's Davy, barefoot, no shirt on, just a pair of pants. He looks at me standing in the bright sunshine. He says, Scags? I say, Yeah, don't you remember me? He sniffles back the snot in his nose and wipes his eyes with the back of his hand. He finally smiles and says, Come in, no one's here but me.

I jump up the stoop into his house and he slams the door behind me. It's unfinished inside his house. The floors are bare, there are boxes everywhere with piles of scrunched up newspapers around them. The boxes look like a maze.

Want to play? I say to Davy. Can you come outside? He shakes his head no, takes my hand and walks with me into the living room which has no drapes, no furniture, just boxes. He pulls me to the far wall. Leaning against that spot is a huge picture of a woman, a dark woman, standing up straight and tall, with a white dress on, red high heels, scarves around her neck, big hoop earrings catching the light. Davy and I stand side by side looking at the picture. Now I see that Davy was crying. His eyes are teary. Who is that? I ask him. That's my mother, Davy says. She sure is pretty. I like her dark eyes. She looks like a gypsy. Davy says, Don't ever tell her that. I ask, Why not? Davy says, She's one of a kind, she doesn't belong to any group, at least that's what she tells me. Do you want to see her room? I figure if he wants to show me the room there must be something really good in it. We climb the stairs that creak when we walk on them. Upstairs our footsteps echo into all the empty rooms. His mother's room is all the way down the hall. It is a shrine to beauty, Davy says.

I feel goofy going into this stranger's bedroom. It is big and white with heavy green drapes over the windows and a long dressing table with a long gold-rimmed mirror. The bed isn't made. Clothes are thrown on a big black chair—a man's pants wrinkled with one leg inside out and a woman's robe, with a big rope belt. The room smells of the peonies in a vase on the nightstand next to the bed. I look around and can't understand why Davy has brought me up here. Some shrine, it looks like a rat's nest as Odessa would say, what with everything everywhere.

Davy goes to the closet and opens the door. I look inside. It is a deep room with clothes, so many clothes all hung up. It smells of leather, all the shoes piled in a hodge-podge as if her feet were too fast to take the time to line up pairs. Davy goes in and walks all the way to the back and comes out holding a black lace bra. Davy holds it over his bare chest and then says, Put it on. I look at the lace, I look at the bigness of it. Davy pushes it against my chest but I start to giggle and say, What do you mean? It's so big. Davy starts to giggle too and holds it up for me to see.

He throws the bra on the unmade bed and grabs my hand. We run down the hall to the creaking stairs, our footsteps sounding like a cavalry charge. We run to the back of the house, to the kitchen still giggling. Davy and I slide down to the floor. He opens a cupboard. Out comes a big bag of Jay's potato chips. He digs deep inside. I hear the crackling, pop, zip of reaching in, coming out with a handful of chips. We eat the whole bag, every last chip and then lick the salt and grease off our fingertips. Davy tries to blow up the empty bag. His chest rises and falls so much he gets out of breath and punches the bag against his chest and says, Here, try it on. I get the giggles and we laugh as loud as we want in the empty house.

The Expressway

It is very early in the morning and I am doing a bad thing. I am eating my breakfast before getting dressed. Odessa isn't saying anything but her eyebrows did shoot up when I came into the kitchen. I finish and go back upstairs and dress on this cool Saturday morning. One, two, three, it is not so hard to get dressed. Pops comes into my room with his finger at his lips. Shush, he means and then dangles his car keys, pulls a baby blue pair of sunglasses out of his shirt pocket and hands them to me. I put them on and ask Pops, How do I look? He smiles and says, Come with me. We go through the kitchen where Odessa is on her knees cleaning the oven and go out into the garage. Pops hits the garage door button. The door rises.

Get into my car, Pops says. I jump in and climb over the seat into the back, where children are supposed to sit and wait for him to get in. He slides into the car and tells me to sit in the front seat with him, that we're going on an adventure. I climb back and seat myself next to him.

We pull away from our house which looks so sleepy now because the drapes are pulled in the living room and dining room. Mama doesn't want the sun coming in and fading the carpet. No other cars are on the street and I ask Pops where we're going. You'll see, he says to me. I love being in the car with Pops until he pushes the button on the radio and I just as quickly shut it off. I don't like to listen to the radio with Pops. He gets all excited and either sings loud with his face shoved out the window or argues with the weatherman.

What are you doing, Scags? Pops asks. I like this music. In my best Mama voice I say, Music is fine but it's not everything. Pops pats my head and says, You win.

Where are we going? I ask as he drives fast out of our neighborhood. He says to me, Would you like to sit on my lap Scags while I drive? I say, Of course I would. Who wouldn't want to sit on his lap and drive down the street with one arm out the window and one hand on the steering wheel? He sits up straight and I crawl in under the steering wheel and now I can see the street and feel the hum of the engine.

Take the wheel, he says to me and with both hands I grab on and steer the car. Pops says, Do you see that Buick with its fish eyes? Think they're driving a shark? A shark? I ask, Yes, I see it. And that blue Chevy pickup, Pops says, Steer clear of him. They could mess up our paint job. We're driving a Chevy too. Pops calls it the peoples' car, indestructible and trustworthy.

Pops slows down the car a bit and then we stop at a light. He looks over my shoulder at the dash. I look too. There's hardly any gas in the tank, I say. He says, Don't be a worrier, there's nothing to worry about. Sometimes Pops drives with no gas for a long time.

The light changes to green and we drive on. Pops lowers my hands on the steering wheel and we turn onto a ramp that goes in a circle. We slide to the right, he slows down a bit more and then we get to the end of the ramp and he says, Drive straight. He takes his hands off the wheel and we are zooming down this straight road I have never seen before. He pushes down on the gas pedal and we are flying along with no other cars anywhere. The wind is blowing my hair in my face and the speed of the car is so fast that I look at the speedometer and we're going 100 miles per hour. I start to laugh. Pops is singing in my ear When the Saints Go Marching In. I keep us on the road. Soon there is a sign I can't read we're going so fast.

Pops takes his foot off the gas and puts his hands on the wheel again. We coast to the right where there is another one of those circles. He says, Get off me now, your butt is too bony. We drive back home, him whistling his song and me thinking what it feels like to drive 100 miles per hour on an empty gas tank with Pops holding onto me laughing and the air, the trees, the bare ground all whizzing by as if we were almost standing still and they were moving.

My heart is beating fast and Pops has that look on his face like he just lit up one of his Cuban cigars and the tip is glowing red and he's had a good day. He says, Don't tell Mama what we've done Scags, you got it?

14

Davy Says

Davy and I are standing King of the Hill on a pile of dirt of an excavation when he says, I know you don't have a thing. A thing? I say. Yeah that thing between my legs, you don't have one. You're a girl. Of course I'm a girl, I say, what did you think I was? Would you like to see a thing? he asks and I ask, Why do you want to show it to me? A thing? I ask, why do you call it a thing? Because I'm being nice to you, he says. Girls get all stupid about things. They giggle and stick out their fingers to touch it. Really, I say, did you show your thing to other girls? Oh lots, he says, where we lived before there were lots of girls who wanted to see it. I say to him, I know a girl doesn't have a thing and doesn't need one but maybe it would be fun to have a thing and show it off to the girls.

Did you ever see your father's thing? Davy asks. I wonder. Did I? I don't know, I say after a long time kicking at the dirt, watching the rocks roll down the side of the hill, trying to remember. Huh, Davy says, you're 7 years old and you've never seen a thing. Have you ever seen a girl undressed, I ask him. Did you ever see your mother undressed? Davy comes up to me and plants a wet kiss on my lips. Even though he's 9 years old that doesn't mean he has to be like this. Hey, I say, wiping his spit from my lips. Hey, I say, what are you doing? He says, Want to be my girlfriend? Why, I ask him, what would be different? Davy says, Then I could show you my thing. He laughs and laughs like Woody Woodpecker.

We're standing so close to each other that I smell his breath like clover and can see the black dots in his brown eyes. He's smiling at me. Davy puts his hands on my shoulders and presses me down, down. We fall to the ground. You'll see, Davy says. All I can think about is how Pops never showed me his thing and what Odessa said about it, how a boy pees and makes babies with it and naturally I would like to see something like that. Like it is a science experiment. It's going to be very educational

Davy unbuckles his belt and lies down next to me. Undo me, he says and takes my hand and puts it on his pants. It's hard trying to unbutton his pants and pull down the zipper with one hand. I do want to see what his thing looks like. Davy's eyes are staring straight at the sky and I see a little brown spot on his neck where he missed when he took a bath.

I'm scared Davy, I whisper, what if someone sees us? Who's going to see us? Davy asks. No one ever sees us. We could be on a ship at sea. We could be Adam and Eve. Who are they? I ask and the zipper opens up. He says, Shut up, don't you know anything? Haven't you been to Sunday School so you could learn about religion? You need to learn about God, he says. Why? I ask. Pops says there is no God. Oh, he says like he never thought about that before, oh, he says, low in his throat, you're going to burn in hell, there's no two ways about it unless you go and learn about God and believe in Him. Well, I don't, I say, and if Pops doesn't believe and he goes to hell, then I'll go with him.

The zipper is open, I say. He laughs at me and says, Took you long enough. He jumps up and pulls his pants and underpants down around his ankles but he's standing with his back to me. I can see his bottom, white, like two little hardboiled eggs sitting on the table. I hear him pee. I lie still on the ground just holding my head up as he pees into the excavation below. I listen to him laughing. When he turns around to show me his thing, his little budding twig all red and pink, I get up and stand next to him. So this is it? I say. Yeah, he says, want to touch it? I point at it and giggle as if this was the tickling game and with my finger I poke it. It wiggles. Davy says, Okay, now you know what a thing looks like. He pulls his pants up and buckles his belt.

We run down the hill together, dirt flies, we yell The Thing, The Thing and giggle all the way to our bikes and ride to his house. Drop the bikes. Jump around yelling, The Thing until Davy's mother comes out of the house with a man and says for Davy to come with them. They walk to the car in the driveway with Davy holding his mother's hand. They leave quickly. I stare down the street watching them go away. I pick up my bike and ride to my house. I leave my bike on the front stoop and go into the back yard and lie down under the cottonwood tree where it is cool and fresh and now I wish I had a puppy to play with. A little baby dog all my own.

Witch's Well

Davy and I are standing in his backyard where I know Odessa can find me to call me in for supper. I tell Davy there is a place where he can go and see things he won't believe. That the place is haunted, that the big kids are the only ones who go there and they only go in groups. They see spooks and the spooks are not human and they can fly.

Nah, he says, what are you talking about? He kicks his toe into the ground where his mother just planted a rose bush and says for me to show him where this place is and he'll go there and see for himself. That I can come too, if I want to. I don't want to, I say. Why, you a chicken, you little chicken, you are chicken, he says. I know that he doesn't know how spooky Witch's Well is and I say, I bet you're scared to go alone and that's why you say I can come too.

I say, A little girl was found in the lagoon one Halloween, a girl from my class, Lizzie Brown. She was in her costume and she was dead and no one knows what happened to her. Who says? he says. I say, Why don't you believe me? Davy says, Because you're scared to go and you're just saying this. I tell him back, real fast, I know more about some things than you do. Lizzie was a friend of mine and she probably went to see the spooks on Halloween and they threw her underwater.

Okay, he says, if I go do you want to come with me? I don't want him calling me chicken again so I say, Yes, after dinner tonight. It's spooky at night, I say, and he laughs at me and calls me a girl.

Odessa's holler finds me and I jump up and then rush home yelling over my shoulder, See you after dinner.

I sit through dinner and let Mama and Pops talk. Money is acting reckless, Pops says about her colored boyfriend. They talk quietly about it so that Odessa doesn't hear how worried they are about Aunt Money. Pops says, It's no good to go squandering her youth, as Mama says, What does anyone do with their youth but throw it away as if there was an endless supply of looks and time. But you don't understand Bev, she is flirting with disaster. Let's change the subject, Mama says, and asks Pops if he has talked to Boomer yet about his new ideas.

Pops shakes his head no. He says, It's not possible yet. I've got to catch him at that right moment when he doesn't think I'm just wanting to leave him because I want to distract him from all the things he thinks

I've done wrong. It's a big step, Bev. We could lose everything. Mama says, I know, and pats her throat and then touches my cheek. She says, Scags when you finish eating go out and play.

I swallow my peas like little green pills. I cut up my meat in tiny pieces so I can chew them quickly. As soon as I finish eating, I say, Excuse me please, and Mama nods. I fold up my napkin, run down the stairs to the basement for the flashlight off Pops' tool bench and then out the basement door I go, running around the house, down the block to meet Davy. I can't be seen going this far from the house at night.

Davy is on the next corner and sees me coming. I run towards him. He turns and runs toward Witch's Well. I yell, Hey wait up. He finally stops at the foot of the hill leading into the woods, and asks, Is this where we go? I say no, this is just the hill, the lagoon is through the woods, down a path. He says, Let's go, and I lead the way.

We get to the top of the hill and I turn to look back at him. He is breathing hard and has a streak of dirt from his eye to his chin. I know it is going to get dark in a little while because I see the sun sitting in the trees. It's hot and buggy and sticky. I smell our sweat. Davy kicks an empty cigarette pack and asks if we're there yet. I say, I don't think so. I point to the path between the trees up ahead and he runs by me. I grab onto his belt and let him pull me along. The trees make a tent dripping with dark spots, lighter spots, birds and flying insects that crash into my head. It is so quiet except for my Keds breaking the twigs and stomping on the leaves. I hear my breathing in my head like big gulps of air, like air was water and I was thirsty.

We get to the top of the hill and the trees arch over us like a blanket about to fall and suffocate us. We don't talk but sit catching our breaths. Davy kicks at the dirt with the toe of his shoe, while turning his head in all directions. Me too. I'm looking for the spooks. I keep scratching the backs of my legs and swatting away the mosquitoes that make a cloud around me. I hear frogs and see June bugs. The light is gone. I squeeze myself up to myself so that nothing is hanging out for anyone to grab onto. I tell Davy to stop making noise so we can hear when the spooks come. He laughs at me, but quietly, and says, No spooks are going to come.

I want to leave. I don't like the hollow sound of the owl. I say to Davy, Let's go. He takes the flashlight from my hand and holds it under his chin and turns it on. He looks like a skeleton with a big grin. He looks black and white and red. His eyes are gone into his head and his nose looks big and looms over his mouth. He grabs me quickly by the shoulder and I scream. I didn't expect that. He puts his finger to his lips and says, Shush.

I hear something. He turns off the flashlight. It is really dark now. We look over the top of the hill where the noise came from and see a light down by the water. I put my hand over my mouth so I'll keep quiet. Davy hands me the flashlight and crawls on his belly over the edge of our hill. I put the flashlight under my chin and follow him on my hands and knees. We crawl very quietly as if we were invisible in this darkness and the spooks didn't want to have anything to do with us. The rocks and stones and dirt dig into my hands and my knees and I feel like peeing.

We're above the light. I hear a boy's voice, then a girl's voice, then another boy's voice. I cannot see who they are. Davy turns to me, puts a finger to his lips, and lies down to watch. I put the flashlight on the ground between us. I know the big kids are there to see the spooks too and they must be waiting like we are to see them rise out of water and go up and up like balloons in the trees. I hear a lot of breathing and then a girl's voice as if she's being strangled, say, slow down, not so fast.

Davy sits up and looks further down and starts to laugh and tries to hold himself back and hold himself back and I feel his laugh. It gets bigger and bigger inside his stomach, his lungs. I look over the edge. I see three naked kids standing up and I know the spooks have taken their clothes and left them to die. Before I can ask him what's so funny about that, he stands up and starts to run. He runs and runs, I chase after him, leaving the flashlight, tripping through the darkness. I fall over and get up, a light comes on behind us and voices call out, Who's there, where are you, but we keep running all the way back to my house.

We run and run until my front yard where Pops is standing on the lawn waiting for me. He laughs when he sees the two of us. Davy is laughing so hard and I'm trying to look like a good girl so he won't know I lost his flashlight and that I went too far from home.

Hey Pops, I say and he says, Scags, let's go inside now. It's getting late. Davy taps me on the shoulder and then runs off. Pops asks, Where have you been? Oh, nowhere, I say. What were you doing? He asks. Oh, nothing, I say, and run into the house ahead of him. Mama is on the phone with Aunt Money, I can tell, and I think, the spooks can't get me now and I'll never be called chicken again.

Mr. Arthur

It is Saturday morning and I leave the house. Mama has gone shopping with Mrs. Arthur. Pops is down in the basement working at his tool bench. Odessa shoved me outside because it is such a nice day. I am on my way to Davy's when I pass by Julia's house. Mr. Arthur is painting the shutters. He has a small white cap on his big head and a pair of torn shoes that are all cracked and without laces, dotted with paint. He whistles, he is always whistling, as if he knew every song ever written. I never know what song is coming from between his lips.

So I say, Hey Mr. Arthur, What's that tune? He stops whistling and looks at me over the tops of his glasses. I see little specs of paint in his raised eyebrows. He says, Some Enchanted Evening, like I should know, but I don't. I like it, I say. He starts to sing in a very deep voice, Some enchanted evening, you will meet a stranger, you will meet a stranger across a crowded room.

He laughs and says, Pretty isn't it? I like Duke of Earl, I tell him and go in a low voice, Duke, duke, duke of Earl. He laughs at me and says, Kids don't have any taste for the finer things. He asks, How are you doing Scags? Do you miss Julia?

Of course I miss her, I say, but I've got plenty to keep me busy. Although a letter from her would be nice.

Yes, Mr. Arthur says, she doesn't like to write letters but she did mention you in her last one and said to say hi.

Where are you going? he asks me. I say, To my friend Davy's house. What are you going to do with him? he asks. We're going bug collecting. Mr. Arthur asks me if I want to help him paint. I look at him on his ladder and I think how Julia says to me that I talk to him too much and listen to his stupid stories. She doesn't like me to do that. She tells me I don't have to live with him and his orders all the time, that stepfathers are no fun because they're not your real father even though she has to call him Dad. Julia says, He's only my Dad because he married my mother. Anyway, she's not here to talk to.

Mr. Arthur isn't from Skokie or Chicago. He's from Brooklyn, which is far away and in another state. I've never been there but Julia and Mr. And Mrs. Arthur go there in the spring for Passover and stay at Mr. Arthur's sister's house who lives in Queens. Wherever that is.

I say to Mr. Arthur, Is Brooklyn big, as big as Chicago? Mr. Arthur whistles a long high pitch and says, Brooklyn is bigger than you know and part of New York and New York is bigger than you know. It has five boroughs and is a different world from Chicago. He stops painting. You'll have to come with us one year. I'll take you to the top of the Empire State Building.

Keen-o, I say and start to walk away. Mr. Arthur asks me, Do you want to hear a story about my first job in Brooklyn? I've never been there, I say and Mr. Arthur says, Well use your imagination. See in your mind miles and miles of apartments. There's a place called Coney Island where there is a huge roller coaster and right there the ocean.

Mr. Arthur says, There was a man named Mr. Slitzky who lived in the apartment building my family lived in. Mr. Slitzky owned the newspaper stand on the corner. He needed a boy early in the morning and late in the afternoon to help him put out papers, make change, and keep the other boys in the neighborhood from stealing candy and fruit. I was a big boy at ten but I didn't grow much after that.

Mr. Arthur says, I didn't want to work but I had no choice. I was the oldest and had three younger sisters. What my father wanted me to do I did. I started working in December and it was cold. I hopped from one foot to the other to keep my blood flowing. I had to leap over the counter and chase down little boys who stole the candy and it was so cold I thought if I had to hit them that my fist would shatter.

Every morning at 5:30 we opened the stand, dragged in the newspapers, unbundled them, set them out, and Mr. Slitzky put the coins for change in the coin box. The people came, all the people on their way to work, in the rain or snow, when it was hot or cold, New Yorkers like their newspapers. The cups of cocoa my mother gave me, one for me and one for old Slitzky, was all he ever ate until lunchtime. He didn't even take one of the candy bars. How did he do that? I loved those chocolates.

Mr. Arthur chuckles to himself as he paints and talks but this isn't really much of a story. Then he says, One morning Mr. Slitzky wasn't at the kiosk waiting for me. I waited a long time listening to people complaining, they wanted their newspapers. I got so cold and angry standing out there that I went back to our building and climbed the five flights of stairs to Mr. Slitzky's apartment and knocked on his door. I heard him yell and scream at me to open what he called the goddammed door. I turned the knob. It was unlocked and I went in. The room was dark and Mr. Slitzky was still screaming. I turned on a light because I was afraid he'd gone off his nut.

He was in bed, flailing his arms around. I walked toward him slowly, making certain to stay out of his reach. Slitzky pointed to the floor. When I looked down there were a pair of legs. I had never seen wooden legs before with shoes and socks on them. He kept screaming at me that he had knocked them down, he couldn't reach them, why didn't I help him? I wanted to but I was frozen in place. He put on his glasses and recognized me and said, Mort, goddammit, hand me my legs. I did, I picked them up, they were heavy and once he had put them on we went to work like nothing had happened and he never mentioned those legs to me again.

Well, that was a better part of the story. I tell Mr. Arthur that I liked his story and he asks me if I wouldn't like to help him paint? Oh no thanks, I say and skip along to Davy's. I think of those legs, those wooden legs with shoes and socks. Why did Mr. Slitzky put socks on, it wasn't as if he was going to get cold feet. I shiver a little bit, like when Boomer runs his finger down my spine. I want to remember the story to tell Pops later who will definitely want to hear what old Mort d'Arthur, as Pops calls him, had to say today.

The Tree House

Davy comes to my front door and rings the bell. I run to the door before Odessa can and I see him standing there, ready to play with me. Through the screen door Davy asks, Do you want to know a secret? Of course I do. He says, The Dietrich's are out of town. So what? I say. Davy says, Well Howie and I have been building a tree house and you and I can finish it. Davy says, If you help, when Howie returns he will let you play there too since you helped to finish the damn thing. Davy has taken to swearing in front of me. It might make his Mama upset if she heard him say what he says, but I kind of like it and he says it so well.

I say, Well I thought we could play catch. He says, Nah, let's go finish this thing and then we can have a secret place to go to.

I go outside and follow him down the walk to where he left his wagon. There's wood and a box of nails and a hammer in it. I get my bike out of the garage. Davy sits on the back, pulling his wagon behind us. I pedal to the Dietrich's. Davy is quiet and heavy. Then he says, It'll be fun to climb in the tree, I'll let you pound in the nails if you can do them straight. I know how to pound a nail, my Pops taught me and I'm no girl, I say. Oh yeah? he says.

We bounce up the curb and go up the driveway. It is so quiet. No one is around. The lawn needs to be cut. I push on the pedals hard to get us into their big backyard. The tree house is all the way in back. I push the bike and Davy drags the wagon up to the tree. It is shady and silent. The trees are black, heavy, dripping still with last night's rain.

Holy shit, Davy says. I say, Now what? He says, Close your eyes. What for? I ask, I know what a tree house looks like. I look at Davy and he's spit up all over his t-shirt. I look where he is looking and I see a man's feet dangling in the air wearing black socks and shiny shoes. I look further up, I see his pants with the crease, his jacket, shirt, tie, his hands in fists and then his head which is jutting on the side. He looks like he is trying to scream.

Who is it? I ask. It's Mr. Silverstein, Davy says. I feel my breakfast in the back of my throat. Mr. Silverstein, I say. Oh shit fuck piss, Davy says real fast and wipes his mouth with the back of his hand. We better get someone, he says, and then says, What if he's still alive? Oh no, I say, he's dead. How do you know? Davy asks and then I scream, Mama, Mama.

We run away screaming together. I don't ride my

bike but push it and run all the way back to my house not stopping screaming for one minute. Davy and I run up my front walk, into the house and I slam the door behind us. It feels cold in the house. I grab Davy's hand and we both shiver. I call Mama, Mama, and she and Mrs. Arthur come out of the basement.

What is it? Mama asks and I run to her and throw my arms around her, but she unwraps me and says, What is it, what's all the noise about, why are you two so pale? Davy says, We saw a man, a dead man, hanging from the tree in the Dietrich's back yard.

Mama looks funny now too. Odessa comes into the hallway and says, What is it? Who's hanging from the tree? Mama says, I'll call the police, give them the address and then we'll go over there. Mama looks like she is going to be sick too. Who is it? Mama asks. I say, It was Mr. Silverstein. I saw his face. Mama says, I've got to go there you two. You stay here. Odessa'll sit with you until I get back. Mama and Mrs. Arthur go in the kitchen and call the police and leave through the back door.

Davy and I sit in the living room for a short while and then the silence we keep is broken by sirens. They come so fast and so loud as if they could wake up Mr. Silverstein. The noise hurts my chest and they just keep coming and coming. I run to the window to see what they look like.

Odessa says, Scags come away from there and grab a shirt for Davy. He doesn't have to sit here all messed up. I don't want a girl's shirt, Davy says. I can see he's trying not to cry.

Through the living room window, we can see the police car, ambulance, and fire truck. Everybody's mothers are standing in the Dietrich's driveway, just standing, not talking, but watching the police bring the body out. The mothers make room for it. I go upstairs and pick out one of my favorite shirts for Davy, it's big on me and I wear it to the beach, so I come downstairs with it to give to Davy and he goes, Shit, it's pink.

Odessa says to Davy, Watch your mouth. Take off that dirty shirt and put this on. You'll go home soon and your mother can clean you up.

Davy says, That man is going to go through the fires of hell for what he did. What is that? I ask and Odessa says, Shush now, no need to rile the dead. But he will, Davy says and then we hear his mother.

Davy, Davy, she calls. She runs up the front walk, her gold earrings catching the sun and comes in the house without even knocking. Davy, Davy. She stands next to the door and he goes running toward her. Odessa walks up to her and hands her Davy's dirty shirt.

What's happening? she asks. Odessa says, A man hung himself. These two found him. Davy sticks his face into his mama's chest and she runs her hands over his head and now he's crying. His whole body shakes and I start to cry and Odessa comes to me and lets me put my face into her, deep into her, into

78

a softness I can't get enough of and I cry big gulps of air that feel like they have goldfish in them so that I start to choke.

Mama and Mrs. Arthur come in the house and look at Davy's mother standing there and say hello to her. Mama is all pale now and her mouth is all puckered up. Davy and his mother look at all of us and Mama says, They saw him, they found him. It's awful. Davy's mother shakes her head, says, Yes, awful, and pulls Davy out of our house. I want Davy to stay. I want to go upstairs and color in the big coloring book Goldie gave me. Davy, I say, but Odessa holds me back and pushes me against her, and says, Let him go, he needs to be with his mother.

Mrs. Arthur says, I'd better go down to Viv's and see if she needs my help with the kids. Mama says, I can't believe it, that nice family, those little twins—I can't stand it. What made him do it? We'll never know, says Mrs. Arthur, and she leaves too.

Mama sits on the couch and Odessa says, Did you see him? Mama says, Yes. Then Odessa takes me over to Mama and tells her to hold onto me for a while and she'll get Mama a glass of wine. Mama says, No thanks, Odessa. I need to call Nate. Take Scags up to her room and stay with her a while.

Odessa's eyebrows pucker together and when we go upstairs she asks, What did you see? I hold tight to her arm. Odessa, I say, was he dead? Yes, she says, he was dead. I saw him in the air with nothing holding him up. He looked scared. Why did he do that? Who knows, Odessa says, who knows what makes people act the way they do. Let's take a nap and try and forget this business, Odessa says as she lies down on my bed and I fall onto her as if she were a cloud that could keep me soft and safe. I say, You know Odessa, sometimes you're my Mama too.

18

Nightmare I

As Pops leaves in the morning to go to work, I look at his shoes. They are black, shiny, and new-looking with a spark at the pointed toe as if he could light a fire under his feet. I ask him if these are new shoes, if they hurt his feet. He takes my hands and dances with me and says, Bully my dear, for new shoes they are fascinatingly comfortable and I'll wear them as long as I live. Okay, I say, you can go now. He kisses me on the cheek and I put my arms around his neck. He says, No no no don't do that and I say, Why not? He pulls his white collar away and I see a big red mark. I say, No Pops. He turns into a skeleton laughing and laughing as if being dead were the funniest thing and I hold my breath and close my eyes. The picture goes away and Pops drinks his coffee black, which he never does, and goes out the door, his feet setting fire to the floor under him.

Mama sits in the living room in Pops' chair and sings Some Enchanted Evening. I go outside but it is raining so I go back inside and there is a man I don't know sitting with Mama, holding her hands. Mama says, Scags be nice now, now you have a new Pops. Odessa is sitting on the couch looking like she just broke the best China Mama has.

19

Bugs

Children live only so long as children, they shouldn't crush things, Odessa says as I scoop one spoonful of Rice Krispies after another into my mouth. The kitchen is full of light. The table sparkles. I pile my spoon high with the crunchy bits of cereal, the milk drips and the only sound beside me munching is Odessa humming God Bless the Child. Where is Pops? Where is Mama? Aren't they ever coming down? I ask Odessa who spent the night with me when we listened to Ella Fitzgerald sing Summertime.

Come on Scags, she says and washes the sink again and prepares to clean the stove. She lowers her voice and says, They were out late last night, having a wonderful time with their friends. Now they have to catch up with them Zs. I want my Pops, I say real low because when Odessa is working she doesn't hear much of anything. I slow down, I stop eating fast, but still I don't hear them so I clear my empty bowl and juice glass from the table. Odessa thanks me and I go outside to the patio.

Davy and I have a collection of bugs. We've caught them and then killed them using carbon tetrachloride. All our bugs sit petrified in one last position as if at any moment they could move but won't. They sit in little jars on the patio. We also have pulled many cocoons off trees and bushes and put them in shoe boxes with twigs and leaves. Davy told me yesterday that he doesn't want to walk through the fields looking closely at the leaves of weeds and grasses for the centipedes, grasshoppers, lady bugs, beetles, praying mantises, and all the other kinds of bugs we catch because he hates to see them die. I love to watch them fighting and trying to get away one second and the next they're frozen in one position never to move again. They will always be dead.

Odessa comes to the doorway, watches me tap each bottle she has saved for us while I count them, count up all the dead bugs and there are 23 jars of dead bugs. Where is everyone.

It's Saturday. Pops has to get up. He has to take me for a ride so we can look at all the cars and so he can give me a nickel for every car I know the name of. He has to let me drive. Mama and Pops have to come downstairs right this minute, by the time I count to ten, by the time I tie my shoes, by the time I spell my whole name backwards. If Julia were home we could go for long bike rides, play the tickling game, run through the sprinklers and sunbathe.

I go further into the back yard where I see Davy's window. The shade is closed. Doesn't he see that the sun is shining, the sky is bright blue and that the grass is so green it looks like one of my crayolas? I lie down in the grass and put my face into it. It smells green and a bug goes up my nose. When I sneeze it comes flying out. Now my nose is all tingly and I think, ugh a bug went up my nose. I won't tell Davy. I just want him to come over so we can take some jars and cotton, cleaning fluid and aluminum foil, which I hand out in little pieces because I don't want to use it all up, and go to the fields behind the Mills sisters' house and catch us some bugs.

It is so quiet outside, you'd think everyone has died or moved away. Maybe some kind of gas leaked out of the ground and only Odessa and me escaped it. Maybe this is a dream and I'll wake up petrified in a jar trying to scream.

I feel the tears bubble up in my eyes and my throat gets tight. I don't want to cry but where is everyone, don't they know I'm waiting for them?

I don't know why but I go to the white shoebox where we put our first cocoon and I think while I'm waiting on everyone, as everyone sleeps and ignores me, Davy too, I'll open the box. I feel something hit the side of the box, I open it, and out flies a monarch butterfly. Bright orange and dark black. It hovers over me, over my head, and I let out a whoop, and the butterfly takes a look around its new life. It flies off to Mama's garden where it sits in the bright sunlight opening and closing its wings, drying them off. It flutters around the tomato plants and hops from one stake to the next. There are no other butterflies flying around and there is no one who saw this but me. The butterfly opens its wings and then flies towards the Cooks' next door, up on their roof. Now I can never capture it again. It disappears and I wonder will I ever be able to describe this to Pops and where is he anyway?

The Chameleon

Pops comes in the kitchen door, home from work, a big smile on his face. I run to him, to have him pick me up, let my feet touch the ceiling and to smell him. Yes. Smell his mouth that has said all those words. I run to Pops but he sticks out his hand to stop me, and says, Guess what's in my pocket? Pops, Pops, Pops, you got something for me. I guess—a bag of candy? A yo-yo? a pack of baseball cards? He shakes his head no and then looks at his jacket pocket where something's crawling and glides slowly up the front of him. It is turning colors, from brown to green against Pops' blue suit as I watch it climb to Pops' shoulder. It has a little blue string tied around its neck. What is it? I ask. Pops says, It's a chameleon. What's that? I ask and jump up and down because I want to know why a lizard is crawling up his jacket and why Pops is giving this to me. It walks all over him with its tongue, its long thin tongue flicking in and out, and its eyes practically hidden by little hoods. I ask, What do I do with it?

It's a pet, Pops says. A pet, I say. Dogs are pets and that's what I want, a little puppy I could put in my pocket and that would stick its little head out and cry. This is ugly. You think it's ugly? Pops asks, and then he says, You should have seen all the kids at the State Fair wearing them on their shoulders. Look at his feet and his long tail and the hooded eyes. It can't make any noise and only wants simple things. It can change its colors to blend in with the landscape whatever it may be so that he is not eaten by anything bigger and faster. Isn't it fascinating? Pops asks. Who knows, maybe if you take care of this we can think about getting a puppy, he says. Don't you think it's cute? No, I say again, he's ugly. Well, he's yours, Pops says, it eats flies so you'll have to catch a few every day and give it some water.

Pops, Pops, I say fast, because he is taking the lizard off his shoulder and putting it on mine, What makes you think that something that changes color would make a good pet? Why can't I have a little puppy instead? Take care of this little guy first, he says, what are you going to name it? I don't know, I say, as he sits lightly on me. What does he do beside change colors? I ask. Pops says he doesn't do anything. He just needs his simple self to be taken care of. You'll see, you'll grow to like him and when you play with him—Play with him I say, can he sit up, can he roll over, can he play hide and seek, can he go for walks with me? Pops says, It's yours, make it a home, you hear, you'll see, something that can change colors can be fascinating.

Pops laughs then. What is he laughing at? Why does he smell like he does, as if he had been to the dairy farm like we did last year on our field trip? The sound of his laughter is different from before, it sounds as if he was a long ways away and going through a tunnel fast to get to the other side where I'm waiting for him, me and Lizzie, that's what I'll call it, and Pops laughs all the way up the stairs to his room where Mama is lying down.

Odessa hands me a shoe box she took off the patio. I tell her, My cocoons were in there. She says, They're dead by now. Punch some holes in the top of the box and get some grass and leaves and twigs to make a home. Leave it in the basement where it's cool. Give it some water. Pops says from the top of the stairs, Look for a fly, feed him a couple of flies. He goes back to Mama.

Why couldn't he bring me a puppy? I say to Lizzie as I settle it down for the night. I go catch a fly, bring it to it. I'm a good fly catcher and I like the way they flutter their wings in my closed hand. It tickles. I put the fly in front of Lizzie's mouth and its tongue whips out, catches it and snaps back into his mouth. Odessa brings the top of a mayonnaise jar downstairs filled with water. Lizzie is settled for the night.

At dinner Pops says, Tell Mama about the chameleon. He is so excited and says to Mama, I got Scags a pet today at the fair. Pops laughs and says, I really thought she'd like it. Well, it's the thought that counts, Mama says, but doesn't look at Pops or me. I really thought she'd like it, Pops says again. So I try to like it.

In the morning I take Lizzie out of its box and take it outside on the lawn, hold onto its little leash and watch it turn from brown to green. Davy calls me from his back yard and I tell him to come over. When he sees Lizzie, he says, I'm going to ask my Mom to get me one. I think maybe I should give him mine because Lizzie gives me the creeps. Its skin is dry and it eats a lot of flies.

The next morning I forget to give Lizzie breakfast or even say hello. Odessa says, Don't forget about your chameleon. I say, I won't, I just need to do something. What might that something be that you would leave that little lizard hungry and thirsty? I don't know what I need to do. I go downstairs and talk to Lizzie, I knock the box around a little and then go upstairs.

The next morning I think Lizzie can wait one more day for its fly and water until one morning when I finally think, why, I'll catch a fly and I trap one between my fingers, I put the buzzing fly in my fist and go open the box to hand Lizzie the fly but its eyes don't open nor its mouth. It doesn't move. I let the fly go knowing Odessa will swat it to death and I pick up Lizzie by the tail. Lizzie is like a piece of brown petrified wood.

I put his stiff body in my pants pocket and go

out the basement door which I'm not supposed to do because it has a special lock on it. It rained last night. The grass is slick like a slip-n-slide because the gardener hasn't been around to cut the grass. I walk to the cottonwood tree. I dig a hole for Lizzie under my rock collection. I have rocks with fool's gold as well as mica and quartz buried back here. Now I put them on top of Lizzie. I scrape the dirt over it and put my rocks on top of the little mound.

Wait until Pops finds out Lizzie is dead. Gosh, I say quietly, Lizzie is under all these rocks and I can't let Pops know I killed it. What'll I say? Should I say how sorry I am? I'm getting all muddy and wet sitting here. I just want to say, if Pops had gotten me a puppy instead of this stupid dead lizard, I wouldn't kill the puppy and maybe I did kill Lizzie but it was a dumb pet. So I say, God, I'm sorry I killed Lizzie, I guess. But Pops should have known better what to bring me. He liked Lizzie more than I did and now Lizzie's gone. I'm sorry. Please have him bring me a puppy next time. Thank you.

Boomer And Goldie

Boomer gives me a microscope which is little and black and sits on my desk like a pudgy king while I look at my hair and then a drop of water under it, and I can barely believe what I see. Boomer sits with me and he is smiling, because he sees I like the gift, and that I am going to be a scientist just like he wanted to be but gave up and became a salesman instead. He sucks on his unlit pipe and makes little gruff noises in his throat, like he was the wolf hiding out at grandma's. I tell him to look, to please look at all the barbs on my hair and to look at all the bugs in the water. He says, You like it, you really like the microscope? I say, Yes, as I close one eye and take a long look at the water. That's great, he says. Then I remember to say thank you.

Boomer and Goldie are here at my house, where they rarely come. Boomer drove them here in his big black Cadillac with the white seats. We usually visit them at their house in Chicago on Pine Grove. I like sitting in their sunroom with Goldie while she sips her tea and reads the paper. I love everything about their apartment, the sunlight in the morning and the long hallway where Boomer and I play catch before Goldie tells us to play outside.

When Goldie lets me stay over we go to Woolworth's and I get a big coloring book, new crayons, a box of colored pencils, and a pad of paper to draw on. I have to bring my own books because Goldie doesn't own any children's books.

But when they come to my house and Odessa is not here, they bring Nellie, their maid, who always makes me big gingerbread men. But Nellie couldn't come this time. Odessa is at home so we'll all have to cook and if only Aunt Money was here, she would know what to make for dinner.

Boomer looks out my window at Pops mowing the lawn. Pops wears a pair of bermuda shorts and his golf shoes. It is hot and sticky. It is a fly buzzing in your nose over and over again kind of day and Pops' face is all red. Mama is yelling at him to stop. Nothing stops Pops.

You know he could have waited to mow the lawn, Boomer says and looks angry. Oh Isaac, Goldie says, he's only got two days off a week, leave him alone. Well, he didn't have to fire the gardener, Boomer says. Goldie says, That's his business not yours. I sit down on my bed and watch Goldie and Boomer stare out the window.

You know, Mimi, he's seemed a little tired lately.

93

A little over eager to make the sale but doesn't have enough energy to close the deal. Well, he looks fine to me, I say and Goldie turns her head to me and says, Your Pops is tops, right? I giggle and Boomer says, Mimi why do you always stick up for that boy? Goldie gives Boomer a funny look like Pops is so wonderful that there is nothing to stick up for.

Scags, dear, Goldie says, let me tell you a secret. Boomer thinks so much of his son that he can't let him go. Your Pops wanted to be a singer, did you know that? And he also wanted to be a dancer, Scags, can you believe that? Boomer says. Goldie says, Isaac, let me finish. When Boomer heard that, that your Pops wanted to go to New York and become a singer, he couldn't let him go, he couldn't say goodbye to him, so when Pops wanted some money to go to New York, Boomer said that he'd have to work for it. So your Pops first said, okay, for a year. But here it is fifteen years later and they are still together making a tidy income.

You mean Goldie that Pops could have been a famous singer and made lots of money—

Whoa, little one, Boomer says. If your Pops had moved to New York he never would have fallen in love with your Mama and there would have been no Scags. Was I terrible to keep him from failure and poverty?

All the times he could have told me this, I think, I think of the way he never said to me that I might not have been born. I miss my Pops. I want him to put away the mower and come inside and let me sit in his lap and smell his breath.

Well, I don't know what's happening about dinner, you two, Goldie says and pats me on the cheek, pulls her hand away and there is a nickel between two fingers. Can I have it? I ask, and she says, It's yours. Goldie goes downstairs and Boomer stares out the window. I can tell that he wants Pops around as much as I do.

Boomer says, Don't say anything to your Pops about what Goldie just told you. It's our secret. Boomer looks at me, and he is smiling again, and says, Do you want to look at a piece of paper under the microscope? Do you want to see what that looks like? Then there is a quiet as the mowing stops, the banging of pots and pans starts up and a fly I could have caught to feed to Lizzie, if it were still alive, tickles my palm and I say to Boomer, Let's look at a fly's wing. I open my hand slowly and pull the fluttering wing off the fly, close my fist again and wait for him to die. How high fly? How sad fly. My pet fly as Pops says whenever he catches one. My pet fly has to die. Boomer looks at me and waits and I come over to the microscope, drop the dead fly next to it, put the wing on a slide and cover it with another slide and we look at it. What good is a fly with only one wing? Boomer asks and we both laugh.

Salt

I'm lying in bed at the end of a hot day. I'm so sick with the salt, I mean, without the salt. I get so dizzy. A few times today I blacked out while chasing after Davy. Mama called the doctor and he said I needed to eat more salt. Yuck. Pops has been away on a business trip with Boomer and he just got home. I hear him on the stairs, one heavy foot after the other. He sees me lying in bed during the day. Even Mama is lying in bed from the heat.

Pops drops his suitcase. He says, What's happened here? Mama's room is dark and so is mine. Odessa comes upstairs and brings me a little blue plate topped with yellow eggs and toast. She says, I put salt on the eggs. I say, I don't like salt. Odessa says to me, You don't have a choice, it's either that or in bed for the rest of the summer sick as you are or sicker. I take the plate and sit up as the room spins. It spins so fast I'm afraid we'll all throw up.

Pops comes into my room and sits on my bed. He

says, Let's call the doctor. I say, Mama called the doctor. What did he say? Pops asks. He said I need more salt in my food. Pops puts his head in his hands and whispers, It's all my fault, Scags, it's all my fault? Why? I ask, why is it your fault? It's all from sweating so much and not having enough salt in me. She gets dehydrated, Mr. Morgenstern, Odessa says, as she takes the empty plate from me and leaves the room.

I tell Pops, Odessa must know, her daughter is a nurse. Odessa and her husband put their daughter through nursing school and now she works in a hospital. I've heard Odessa tell Mama that she is dating one of the doctors, but Mama tells Pops there wouldn't be any colored doctors in the hospital. I want to tell Odessa that Aunt Money is dating a colored man. Wouldn't it be wonderful If Aunt Money's boyfriend met Odessa's daughter and they fell in love and what if Aunt Money dated the doctor? This sure seems like such a good idea that I tell it to Pops and he pulls his hands away from his head and places both of them on my face. What a stinking little genius you are Scags. But Pops, there's more to say so take your hands away. He lets go of my face and I feel the cool air wipe my cheeks. You see Pops, I say, if you get sick now like Mama and me and get it over with, then there won't be anymore sickness for a long time. We will have used up our sick genies and can now have only healthy genies. They will laugh with us because we are so healthy. Don't you want to get sick? Don't you want to let Mama and me take care of you?

Is it so much fun being sick? Pops ask me. He pushes my hair off my forehead. I see him staring at his hand when he takes it away. I'm really not so sick now, I say, I'm going to get better right away.

He looks closely at his hand and turns it up and down. I grab it saying, What is it Pops? He turns his face away as if he was crying. I don't hear any sobs but he is definitely crying and I don't know what to do.

Odessa comes back into my room carrying a bowl of popcorn she made for me. She says, It's got plenty of salt and butter on it, just the way you like it. I think, being sick can be fun. Why doesn't Pops want to get sick like Mama and me? He pulls his handkerchief out of his back pocket and blows his nose. Odessa takes a look at him and leaves the room. Pops turns back to me and sticks his hand, his big hand, into the bowl and grabs a fistful of popcorn, opens his mouth wide and tries to put his whole fist in at once.

I start to laugh at him, I laugh and laugh until his mouth is full. He looks funny. His cheeks are like a chipmunk's and his mouth is like a fish and his eyes, his eyes must hurt him he is staring so hard at me. But he shakes his head, stands up and is gone, chomping away on the popcorn. Waving his hand at me from behind his back like it is a tail. He goes to Mama and closes their door.

New Car

I hear loud honking like three notes saying here I am, playing over and over. Mama is in the kitchen talking on the phone to Aunt Money. I run from Mama's side to the living room window to see what's making that noise. Oh. It's Pops. He's sitting in a little red car. It doesn't have a top and Pops sits behind the wheel real low, wearing a white sporty hat.

I yell to Mama, Come see what Pops bought. What? She asks, and I say, A sports car. He what? Mama says, and then tells Aunt Money she'll call her later, and goes out the garage door with me right behind her.

Mama runs straight through the garage towards the car as if she were going to throw herself over it and give it a big hug. Nate? What have you done? she asks and turns to look in the garage. Her car is missing. Where's my car? she asks and Pops just sits behind the wheel, looking up at her, looking up and smiling. I go to the side and watch Mama and Pops.

This is your car, Bev, Pops says, get in and you too

Scags, we'll take a spin. Oh, Pops, I say, running my hand down the red fender that is so shiny that the sun is orange in it. I say, Oh Pops, can I have a car like this when I get big? No one is going to have this car, Mama says, and to Pops she says, Take it back. I want my old car. But I thought, Pops begins to say, when Mama says, You thought wrong. I like my car. But this is your new car, Pops smiles when he says that. Mama says, Think for a moment before you do things Nate. Think, can't you?

I hate it when they argue. Why is Mama so angry? Come on Bev, admit it, you like this car, Pops says smiling all the time, touching his cap, squinting in the sun. How could she not like it, look at it, it's got white seats, a wooden steering wheel, no top and so shiny. How could Mama not like this car?

But Mama turns around and walks back inside the house, fast, holding her hand to her mouth. She walks through the garage and slams the door.

Pops, I say, why is Mama so angry at you? Pops says, She's not angry. Mama really doesn't like surprises. It was a big surprise, wasn't it, he says. She'll be fine. He takes my hand and says, Hop in, we'll take a drive and—And what? I ask. He looks at me as if he had no idea what he was going to say. He stares at me now, as if I knew what he was thinking. He stares and stares and when I say, Pops, Pops, let's go and I slide into the seat that feels molded to fit me, he claps his hands and then pinches my cheek and revs the engine as we pull out of the driveway.

The motor makes a big noise like it could go fast. I ask Pops if I can drive and Pops pats the steering wheel and says, Not this time old sport. But when I get bigger and learn to drive, can I have a car like this? Pops takes the white cap off his head and puts it on mine. I feel like a race car driver. We have no top. We have no windows. Just the windshield between us and the road. I want to go fast, really fast and see what it feels like, so I say, Hey Pops, give it the gas.

Anything to please a lady, Pops says, and off we go down the street, a sharp right then a squealing left and maybe we're on our way to the expressway. We drive in traffic and it feels like we're floating in air. Everyone must be jealous of us and think we are the luckiest people to have a red sports car with white seats and a wooden steering wheel.

Pops is still smiling but not humming and he pulls the white cap over my eyes. I pull the cap up and look at where we're heading, into a car lot where there is a parking space that looks so tiny only my Pops could fit in there. Pops pulls the car in and shuts off the engine. He tells me to get out. My legs are stuck to the seat and sound like pants ripping as I pull myself up. I get out of the car and follow Pops around a building where sitting all alone is Mama's car. We get in and drive home.

Bowling I

Pops is home early on this hot night. Pops likes to drink beer when it's hot. Mama says to him, Whoa, where's the fire? Because Pops has drunk 4 beers. Pops laughs and says to Mama, You just don't understand and I don't have the time to explain to you that it's hot and the heat does strange things to a man. The beer is sooo cold and when you're ready to join me, I'll gladly share this beer with you.

He lines the empty bottles up under his chair in the living room. He has moved all the furniture to one side so he can have a clear shot at the fireplace with the bottles which he bowls into it, the swept-out, brick-lined hole in the wall where every winter Pops builds fires, big fires and we sit close together as if we needed to keep each other warm.

Mama says, You shouldn't drink so fast, slow down, come eat dinner. Pops laughs again and waves his arms in the air like a broken helicopter and says, You eat, I'm not hungry.

He stands up and takes one of the empty bottles from under his chair, holds it on its side, takes two long steps and bowls it into the fireplace where the glass explodes and is so loud that I have to put my hands up to my ears. I run to Pops and grab his arm but when I look at his face, he looks right at me and says, I like this crash, bang, crack of broken glass. I don't say, Well I don't as he puts the cold one to his lips and I watch the lump in his throat rise and fall as he swallows it all down.

He pushes me away from him and turns to Mama and says, Your turn. What does anyone want to do that for? Odessa asks and picks up the empty bottles and starts to walk away with them when Pops yells, Those are my bottles. I never heard this voice before. How can he talk like this, to be so mean and loud? How can he be mean to Odessa?

Odessa turns to him and says, Mr. Morgenstern are you yelling at me? Pops' face has a look on it like you better believe it. His eyes are so dark, how have they come together and he's thinned his lips so that there is a big splash of black and a little splash of red on his face and he's holding the empty bottle in his hand by the neck and Mama holds herself together by wrapping her arms around herself. I say, Pops why are you like this? I thought you were having fun.

Fun, Pops says, who says anything is fun anymore? Huh? Huh? He walks toward me holding the bottle in one hand and with the other he grabs for me like he was blind. I run, I run out of the room and sit on the stairs. Pops says, This is my house, you'll let me do what I want.

Put those bottles down, Odessa, Pops says. I hear the clink of glass, and Pops smashes another, then another, then another into the fireplace. I feel like those bottles are crashing in my head. Who is Pops tonight?

Scaaags, he yells and I put my hands over my ears and run up the stairs, close my bedroom door, and lie on my bed with peppery tears rolling out of my eyes. This is worse I think than when he punished me for coming home late from Davy's. Then he sent me to my room and then went out and bought me a deck of cards with trains on them. I go to my desk and look for them, but I can't find them, I can't find them. This is worse and if he comes up here looking for me, I have no where to hide. I get up and listen at the door. No sounds. I open the door slowly, it's dark in the hall but there he is standing so quietly. I hear Mama and Odessa behind him on the stairs.

What do you want to scare Scags for? Odessa asks. He grabs for me and holds me to himself. He is crying and I can feel his body shivering. I don't know what's wrong with me, Scags, Pops says. Mama says, You're drunk, Nate, leave Scags alone and let's eat.

I'm shivering too. Pops' eyes are all bloodshot and I want to think how he is better now. He can only be mean once and then he will be nice, very nice.

Crab Apples

I tell Davy that Julia is really my best friend and I keep wondering when oh when is she going to come home? What do you want to have her for? Davy asks, when you've got me? I am perfectly aware of you, I say to Davy in my best Mama voice, but a girlfriend is different from a boyfriend.

I'm not your boyfriend, Davy says, and sits down on our front stoop next to me. He has a little knife that Jack, his mother's boyfriend gave him, he is whittling down a thick twig to a sharp point so he can make an arrow out of it. Your Mama has a boyfriend, right? I ask and Davy nods his head yes. Then why can't you be my boyfriend? I ask. Because I don't want to get all mushy with you, you're just a kid. Oh, I say, and wish Davy would go away and play with some other kid. I feel tired and want to take a nap on the grass under my tree.

Davy says, I know where we can go and get some good crab apples. I say, So do I smartie. He says, Don't be so piss-filled with yourself. Davy still thinks swearing is keen-o. Whenever I tell Odessa what Davy says to me she says his mother ought to wash his mouth out with soap and that if he had a proper home he wouldn't be like that.

Crab apples, Davy whispers into my ear, I'll race you, he says. I jump up and run as hard as I can down the block towards the Mills sisters' house. They have lived there forever in their yellow brick house and rarely come outside. I love crab apples and so does Julia. I almost beat Davy to the crab apple tree, but I slip on the grass at the corner of their yard and start to scream when Davy puts his hand over my mouth. Yes, I remember, I must be very quiet or else we'll be caught. They don't like us kids coming into their yard at all. Davy picks from the branches, I pick up hands full off the ground, off the grass, and stuff them in my pockets after making sure they have no worms in them.

When my pockets are full, I whisper to Davy, Let's go. He has been eating as many as I have picked up and he still wants to fill his pockets. I pull a green and red one from the branch above my head. I bite into it and it makes my cheeks suck in and my tongue tickle. We hear the Mills' black scottie barking and we run away because we're afraid they'll yell at us. I hear the sucked in breath of a door opening and a racket of birds fly away. Davy and I run, run, run. I hold my pockets and let my legs push me further and further away from the crab apple ladies.

We return to my front stoop all out of breath and smiling at how we tricked the old ladies and got what we wanted and didn't get yelled at.

Do crab apples taste that good? I ask Davy. I put one in my mouth and another one, each in a pocket of my mouth and then spit them out. I put them on my chest under my shirt.

I twist my body back and forth at Davy but he doesn't seem to notice that now I have breasts. But then he says, Hey, where'd you get those knockers? Can I touch them, he asks and I say, Sure but just with one finger. He raises his hand in the air and then points his pointer at my chest and before he can touch them they fall down. Davy holds his finger in front of my shirt as if he can't believe what happened and then says, Well that might have been good for a laugh.

If I wear them there all the time, I ask Davy, will you be my boyfriend? What do you want me for? he asks and takes out his knife and begins peeling one of the apples. You know, Davy says, boyfriends are tricky. Sometimes they say they love you just to get you into bed. How do you know that? I ask and wonder why they'd want to go to sleep.

My mother has had a lot of boyfriends, Davy says, and then says, It seems like a lot of work to be a boyfriend. Why? I ask him, it's okay if you don't want to be my boyfriend but why is it so much work? Davy says, Well, you have to be on time, bring gifts, take the girl out to fancy restaurants. You've got to look good and be clean all the time. Jack said to me that wooing a girl is harder than being president.

But we're already friends. Yes, Davy says, put those apples under your shirt again. I do. They stay. He touches and smiles. Davy says, That was nice, let's go to my house? What for? I ask.

You know what those old ladies do in that house all day long, don't you? Davy asks and then laughs. I ask him, Why are you laughing? Don't you know that those two old ladies aren't sisters and that they eat pussy?

I haven't the tiniest, littlest, teeniest idea what he is talking about or why that is so funny. I never knew you could eat cats and I wouldn't want to. I don't want to let on that I don't know and I say, Of course, everyone knows that about them, it goes on all the time. I cover my mouth with my hand and pretend I am laughing too.

You don't know what you're talking about, he says to me, but you could find out. How? I ask. His mouth is full of apples, his eyes all crinkled up. Then his mother calls his name and he spits the apples out of his mouth into the shrubs, runs around my house, jumps the hedge and is in his back yard where he puts his hands on his mother's hip before I have time to say wait for me.

I stand up and she waves to me and her gold earrings shine and then the two of them walk away together and I say to myself, when Julia comes home

I'll ask her what eating pussy means. I'm not letting Davy Armstrong know I'm a complete idjit as Goldie says whenever Boomer says something she already knows—what do you think I am, a complete idjit?

Ribbons And Bows

Mama is all excited. Mrs. Arthur invited her on an outing, they are not going to use their coupons, no, they are going to a fashion show at a hat store in the city. It is Sunday and Pops says he has nothing to do, so he wants Mama to stay with him, maybe take a drive and get some ice cream and look at some new houses. We're not moving anywhere, Nate, she says and fusses in her room with lipstick, rouge, powder and her hair, of course. Her hair is jet black which she wears short around her neck and sometimes Pops, to be mean, says she looks like a boy. But that's not fair because she is so beautiful that way. When Mama turns from her mirror to look at us I see how she really does look like a queen which would make Pops a king and me a princess.

Mama leaves in a swirl of perfume and scarves. I go to my room, turn on my lamp, put some salt on a slide, cover it with another slide and look through my microscope. I see an ice palace like we try to build in the winter, me and Pops.

I hear the garage door going down and I yell out Pops, Pops. No Pops. He's gone. Did he forget I am home? Well hell's bells, as Davy would say, and I go downstairs looking around. All the doors are open. The light is on in the kitchen but when I look out the door to the garage, Pops' car is gone. Mama's Chevy is there. Why Pops? You left me alone. I've never been home by myself.

I slam the door shut then run scared to the front door and slam it and run into the kitchen and slam the basement door and run up to my room making as much noise as I can. There may be spooks outside that are now inside. I can scream unless they choke me.

I must entertain myself, as Mama would say. But I don't want to. I can't go outside because then no one would know where I am. I slam my bedroom door. The whole house is empty. I look at my bookshelf next to my dresser. Odessa has arranged my books again. I see a baby book that Pops used to read to me, the one where a crow learns to speak and tell the future to a king who doesn't want to believe the crow because crows can't talk.

I open the book and see once again the black crow with his big wings and serious look in his eyes. I go to my desk and push the microscope aside and pull out some drawing paper. I say to myself, when the picture is done, Pops'll be home. I can hardly wait to finish. I take a piece of brown paper and draw the head of the crow, with its big beak and its angry eyes and I think I could draw another picture of it flying and its wings extended so far that he looks like a little airplane.

But no Pops. So I lie down on my bed. My pillows are so soft. If I put my face in one of them no one will hear me cry but there is no one anyway. I know if I lie perfectly still and don't think anything, everything will be okay. I hold my breath a few times to listen to nothing. I wait for some sign that everything is going to be okay. Maybe—-the doorbell rings.

It rings again and I jump off my bed, run down the stairs to see who's there. I swing open the front door and there is Pops. Why is he standing there? Why doesn't he come in, it's his house after all and why did he leave me all alone?

I hear a voice that is not Pops'. I yell, Who's there? I see a man standing behind Pops wearing a uniform. It's a policeman. Your mother home? he asks and I say no one is here but me. What do you want with my Pops? Is this man your father? he asks me very seriously and I open the screen door and throw my arms around Pops and they walk in the house, me hanging onto Pops, him walking with me standing on his shoes.

What's wrong Pops? I ask him. He smiles a little smile like not to worry. He says he left without his wallet and when he went to the store to buy me some new ribbons for my hair he had to put them in his pocket he was so embarrassed not to have any money. Pops says, Go to my room and get my wallet.

I run upstairs thinking, is Pops a crook? Well no, and anyway he's home now and everything's going to be fine. I run back downstairs with Pops' wallet to show the policeman that my Pops is no crook.

Pops clears it all up. The policeman leaves and Pops and I are alone in the house. It is so quiet that I can hear the refrigerator purring in the kitchen. Pops says, Guess what I got you? He pulls red ribbons, brown barettes and pins out of his pants, saying, They didn't find these. He is laughing. I ask, Did you really steal these? He says, Yes. I ask him why, but all he says is, Go get your hairbrush. I run to my bathroom, and he calls up the stairs, Get the brush and a pair of scissors to cut the ribbons.

Pops is in his chair drinking a beer when I come back downstairs. Stand with your back to me, he says, and puts his beer down but first he offers me a sip and I say, No thanks, I don't like the taste of beer, I stand between his legs, with my back to him. He pulls on the elastic Mama put in my hair this morning, but it is stuck because Mama can't do it as well as Odessa. It hurts as he pulls it and I start to cry, but only a little bit. Don't worry, Pops says, give me those scissors, I'll cut the elastic off. I hand them to him and I hear the scissors snipping and snipping. It's not that hard to cut an elastic. He tells me to turn around.

I face Pops. In his hand is my hair, all my long red curly hair. I run my hand down the back of my head and I don't know what to say. To do. Where to look.

At the hair in his hands or the stare in his eyes. Pops looks away from me. What did he do to me?

Go away, he says, and places my hair in his lap and reaches for the beer. Leave me alone, he says, now, right now.

I run upstairs and go into his room and slam the door. I sit down at Mama's makeup table and stare at myself in the mirror. I need to see the back. I need to see what he did to me. I cry softly, Why Pops, why Pops? Look at me. Look at me. I look like a boy.

I pat my head and stop crying. I reach into Mama's top drawer and pull out her white and green chiffon scarf and wrap it around my head and then my neck. I could wear my blue sunglasses and my mint green sun dress. I will still be pretty. As pretty as a peach, Pops didn't mean to do this. I shouldn't have let him fix my hair. I'll tell Mama I did it. I cut off my hair.

Hot Dogs

Odessa has made a fire in the grill outside on the patio. Davy and I are going to cook hot dogs for lunch. Pops has whittled some sticks to a sharp point. We have to put them through the cold hot dog and then hold them over the fire. I pull one of the patio chairs, my favorite one because I can lie down on it if I want, over to the grill which is made of bricks and is where Pops cooks chicken and steaks. Oh, yes, I remember, there was one Christmas day he cooked steaks out here wearing his warmest coat and his biggest gloves and a stocking cap, a red stocking cap.

The coals are dark red now and yellow, they send up a wall of heat. I can't see it but I can feel it as I put my hand out to the fire. It feels like my skin could just shrink up like paper in fire.

Look Davy, I say, the fire is winking at us. It's like a blinking traffic light, first red, then yellow, then red. The red is so hot and the coals have white rings around their edges and I can smell the lighter fluid

Odessa used to start the fire. Davy is racing his new blue matchbox car over the sides of the grill. Whew, he says, that sure is damned hot. It feels like it could burn my face off.

Come sit with me, I say, and make room on the chair for him. Sit here, I say, and you won't get burned. He sits next to me and runs his car up my bare arm to my shoulder onto the side of my face and then over the top of my head. He doesn't say anything about my new hair cut. Don't do that, I say. He stops, puts the car down and says, Well what do you want to do?

Odessa comes out to the picnic table, the redwood table with its two benches, and puts out a couple of plates and a big pitcher of lemonade and a bottle of ketchup. As she goes back inside she says, Tell me when that fire is ready for your hot dogs.

Davy watches her go and then says, Want to see something neat? He digs deep into his back pocket. He pulls out a square package, holds it in the palm of his hand and presents it to me. What's that? I ask. I look him straight in the eyes. He has on his I-know-better-than-you smile. He giggles and closes his fist around it. What is it? I ask. If you're going to show me something but not tell me what it is, you're no fun. I'll tell, he says, if you promise not to tell anyone. I say, I won't tell a soul.

Odessa brings the hot dogs and buns outside along with Pops' sticks. Davy giggles through his nose when he sees the plate of franks. They are big and red. Odessa asks, Do you want me to put them on the sticks for you and cook them? I say, No thanks, just help me a little. Odessa picks up one of the hot dogs and pushes the stick through it until it comes out the other end. Davy is laughing and giggling as he does the same thing. Odessa asks him what's so funny and why is he laughing so hard? Davy ignores Odessa and tells me nothing too. Odessa says, after she hands me the stick, Be careful by the fire. She goes back inside looking over her shoulder at Davy and shaking her head. Finally, he gets his stick in the hot dog right and is waiting to cook it.

Davy, I say, what's so funny? He says, Do you want me to show you my secret? I say, Yes. He puts his stick on the table, pulls out the package and opens it. It's little and round. He puts it on the tip of his hot dog and rolls it down until it is all covered by this tight balloon.

He has a very serious look on his face like he's thinking hard about what he's doing. You have to be careful, he says, not to rip it. Once the balloon is over the hot dog, he picks it up and points it at me. He says, I've got you covered. I don't know what he means. He looks at me and says, You don't get it, do you? This is a thing. The hot dog? I ask. Yes. And the balloon? That's a rubber. What's that? That's that, he says pointing. Men's things can make babies inside a woman. I know that, I say. Well smartie, he says, this rubber keeps the man's sperm from getting in the woman. Why? I ask.

What do you mean why? Why don't they want to have babies? I'm all confused. What does Davy do with these rubbers when he's alone? I think if things are something thing Davy has and I don't, why didn't I get a thing? Look at all the neat things you can do with one.

You ready to cook yours? Davy asks as he rolls the rubber off and shoves it in his back pocket. He walks over to the grill, places his hot dog above the flame and turns it ever so slowly to cook it all the way around.

Odessa comes out and sees me staring at Davy's hot dog which is getting plumper and redder. Don't you want to cook yours? She asks me. Stick your hot dog in the fire. I want to wait a little longer, I want to see Davy's hot dog get burnt and then I can put mine in the fire, I say to Odessa. Davy giggles and pulls his hot dog out of the fire and Odessa takes it from him and wraps a bun around it and pulls it off the stick. Okay Scags, she says, I've got some other work to do so you hurry up, you hear?

I slowly get out of my chair and shove my lunch into the fire and put it where it's the hottest slowly turning it like Davy did. I smell all the different smells in the meat, the garlic and the juices. I look at Davy who is stuffing his face, taking big bites of the red, red meat, now dripping with ketchup. I think that Davy's laughing at me because he has a thing and I've only got a hot dog.

Cocker Spiegel

It is Saturday morning and Julia should be coming home soon, maybe today, I don't know when really. I go out to the garage through the kitchen door and jump up and hit the button and the garage door rises and I take my bicycle out, then go back, jump up, hit the button, and run like a bunny to get out of there before the door closes all the way.

It is hot, my gosh, so hot that the sidewalk hurts my feet and the street is so dusty that when the wind blows, the dirt gets between my teeth and crunches in my mouth. I hate this. I take my bike to the end of the driveway and hop on and ride around the block to see if anyone else is outside yet.

On the next street a house with a tiny little yard has a sprinkler going. I ride back and forth through it as the water swishes and I get wet. It feels good and the water streams into my eyes and I can't see and I ride away from there shaking my head, my new short hair making the water fly around me and taste cold and sweet.

Mama says that no one has to brush my hair in the mornings now. Mama calls me her little carrot top. She runs her fingers through what's left of my hair and sighs and says, Oh Scags, I'm so sorry. I say, Pops can't look at me yet but he will. He'll make things all right again. I know he will.

I decide to ride to the drugstore and I check my pocket to see if the dollar bill Boomer gave me is still there. It is but it is wet. Well, Mr. Ruskin will take it anyway, I say. I push hard on the pedals to get to the drugstore just as it is opening.

The candy is right under the cash register. I want a Three Musketeers because it lasts a long time and some Pez for my Mickey Mouse Pez dispenser, I get lemon and orange, and I want one more thing but I don't know what.

There's so much, so much to think about until Mr. Ruskin says, Scags, you can come back again, why—but I don't listen to adults when it comes to candy, they don't know a thing. They say, Get just one thing, but how is that possible when they bring you someplace that has fifty things? I finally decide on a Snicker's bar.

I put my candy up on the counter which is hard to reach. I think Mr. Ruskin is angry at me because I didn't listen to him, but he's not. He asks me if I want a bag and I say yes. I like to put my little parcels in the basket on the front of my bike and drive along so that they don't bounce out.

I give him the wet dollar and he smiles at me and hands me my change which I stick in my wet pocket. It doesn't matter if pennies, nickels, dimes, quarters get wet. Bye, I say, and raise a hand like an Indian and go outside, put the bag in my wet basket and get on the bike for the ride home.

I go to the back yard with my bag of candy. I go to my tree where my rock collection sits on Lizzie's grave. As I'm walking across the grass, I see a mound behind the tree. The mound is crying. I get scared, who is it, what could it be, and then I know and I run to the tree and stop in my tracks.

Five puppies all black and wet sucking on their mother's nipples. All for me, I think. The mother is licking each one of them as they suck and they have such tiny bodies and such tiny eyes that aren't open yet and they must have been born last night.

A dog and five puppies and they're all mine. I found them. They are so cute, little and black. They have these pink tongues and I start to cry when one of them loses the nipple. I go running into the house to get a bowl of water for the mother. I leave my bag of candy on the counter and carry the bowl carefully. When I put it down, she takes a lick of it and looks at me with tired eyes and shuts them and all five puppies are alive and sleeping now too and I run back inside to get my Pops.

Pops is in the living room in his chair wearing

nothing but a pair of bermuda shorts. I tell him I found the puppies and he says, What puppies? The ones in the backyard, I say. He looks at me as if he doesn't understand, but then he remembers and says, We've got to get them covered up because there's going to be a storm tonight, a bad storm. I tell him they are all black and little and just born and exactly what I wanted. He goes and gets a pair of shoes but doesn't put them on but follows me outside in his bare feet.

We have to be very calm around the mother, he says, and we have to see if she'll let us move her, she may not. I have to be prepared for that. I tell Pops that I already brought her some water and she is so tired she can hardly drink. I know there is no talking to a dog, Pops says, but if we are gentle with her maybe she'll let us take her somewhere else.

Where Pops, where can we take her? To my room? I know that is a mistake. I shouldn't let him know yet that these are for me that he is going to give me a puppy because I've been so good and he knows I can be a good girl and take care of them all. All of them. For me.

He bends over the mother and her babies and says, Shush, shush. She opens her eyes, darts them to me, she looks scared. Pops says for me to go to the garage and bring the wagon. I run across the yard and practically trip on myself I'm so tangled up with joy. I guide my wagon carefully so that it doesn't scratch Mama's car. Then I race back to where the puppies are. There is a man with Pops. Pops puts his hand up for me to slow down and be gentle.

Someone I don't know is squatting down with the dog and her pups. I don't like the looks of this. When I get up close I hear the man say, She got in with a beagle and she's full cocker. Pops says, So this makes the pups cocker spiegels. They laugh but I see nothing to laugh about. What does this man dressed in green shorts and a t-shirt and mocassins want with my pups?

Pops sees the look on my face and says, Now Scags, this man owns the dog and these puppies are his too so we're going to let him pick up the mother dog and the babies and wheel them home in your wagon. I look at Pops and he reads my mind. No, he says, they're too young to take from their mother. We'll see about getting you a puppy another time. He seems to have forgotten that I found these puppies under my tree and that makes them mine.

I'm angry at Pops and I drop the handle of the wagon and stomp back to the house and slam the door and walk like I'm wearing cement boots up to my room. The pillow is a good place to scream. So I scream, No fair, no fair. Mama comes into my room. I hear her say, Now Scags, what's happened now? I don't want to tell her because no grown up is ever going to give me what I really want.

The Storm

It is 5:00 but the sky is as dark as night. Pops sends Davy home before the storm hits. Pops says, Before all hell breaks loose. But you, Odessa, he calls from the living room into the kitchen, you must stay. I am sitting at the kitchen counter while Odessa pulls the candles and the candle holders out of the cupboard and places them all in front of me like a band of tulips before they bloom. Pops is very excited. He runs from room to room carrying his flashlight and his transistor radio. Mama walks in the door from the Arthurs' and is full of her smell of cigarettes and wine. Pops walks up to her and takes her hand and says to her, We've got to be prepared. He walks with her into the kitchen. Odessa, Mama says, I thought you'd be long gone by now. Pops says, She has to stay with us, we can't let her get caught in the storm.

Odessa keeps pulling out candles and placing them on the kitchen table, the dining room table and in Pops' bathroom on the first floor. When she finishes we are all still standing in the kitchen. Odessa says, If the power goes out this place will look like a church.

Don't open the refrigerator anymore. Let's keep it as cold as possible, Pops says to Odessa. We can cook in the fireplace if it goes on too long, I think, there is plenty of everything in my house. Just as if Pops could read my thoughts he starts to sing, Oh I've got plenty of nothing and nothing's plenty for me, and then he runs upstairs to make sure all the windows are closed.

When he comes back to the kitchen he slams the back door shut and stares out the window. Mama goes up to him. I wonder about those puppies and wish I had one now. Now would be a good time for a puppy. If it could sit in my lap and lick my face and sleep with me.

Mama puts her arms around Pops as he faces the yard. He pulls away and then turns to grab her by the waist. Pops says, Do you want to dance? Are you all right, Nate? she asks. She takes a step away from him as if it hurt her to look at him. Pops says, Let's go on a vacation. Just the two of us. What about me? I ask. Pops doesn't hear me, he pulls Mama to him and gives her a big kiss.

Odessa says, Come on Scags, we'll go sit in the living room. We'll be fine. I take Odessa's hand and go with her and whisper, Are they going to be mushy all night? I certainly hope not, I answer myself. We sit down on the couch and look out the window together. Look Odessa, I say, the sky is like split pea soup. It's very scary, I say and push myself up to Odessa who puts her arm around me and I can feel how tired she is, how she kind of rests against me too. This won't be too bad, remember the storm last year when your basement flooded?

Pops walks into the living room. Mama is holding his hand and trying to guide him to his chair. He says, There's nothing to be afraid of here. He says, You're covered. He sits down. Don't be shy. Don't cry. Don't wave bye bye. The storm will rattle you to your very bones, shiver and shake miladies. He stands up with his back to us at the window. He's holding his hands and arms like a batter at the plate waiting for the pitch. Hey batter, he says, laughs at something, maybe the pitcher he sees in front of him. Show me your best stuff, Pops says and takes a swing and whirls around himself and almost falls against the glass.

The wind is getting very strong. The hollow spot in the corner of the house moans. Pops goes back into the kitchen, he returns with his radio. Mama sits with Odessa and me. Pops tries to find a station that isn't filled with static. He places the radio to his ear and sits down on the floor. Look at me, he says, I'm in my tailor position.

I look at Odessa's face, her eyebrows pulled down tight now, her big black eyes staring someplace that isn't here. She clicks her tongue and shakes her head back and forth at whatever thought she has and a bright flash of lightning fills the picture window. Right away there is a crash of thunder.

The storm is right over us, Pops says and jumps up. The lights go out. He takes his flashlight and places it under his chin and walks to the dining room table and puts the candles on the buffet. He jumps onto the table and begins to dance. He's too tall to stand up straight. Mama tells him to get off the table but he shuffles his feet from side to side. Mama goes to the table, stands in front of him, reaches her hand to him and again the thunder rattles the house, it rumbles through us as if we were all on a roller coaster just starting down the steep hill.

Odessa's body vibrates. She must be humming something but I can't hear her. She says to me, We're really in the midst of it now.

Pops jumps off the table. It is so dark I can see only the shadows of Mama and Pops. He says, It's like an orchestration, don't you think? Pops looks at me and says, Want me to conduct the storm?

I can't look or hear him anymore. Where is my Pops? Why is he standing in front of the window again throwing his arms as if they had no joints and as the storm gets louder and louder he moves wild and wilder.

Branches are torn from trees, rain drops fall on rain drops and make a racket as if they were hurting each other. Mama tells Pops to get away from the window, get away, she says, come on, we've seen enough of you looking like Moses waiting to receive the word of God, but now it's time to settle down.

Settle down, Pops says, is that all there is on your mind? Where is passion, desire, lust, music, you know what I mean. Where are all the songs I used to know? Pops begins to cry. I hear him sob and with each lightning bolt he is lit up, his arms over his head, his back to us, gone far away and I dig deeper into Odessa's lap.

Mama sits next to me and looks at her hands. Pops turns to talk to us, faces us, bent at the waist as if we were all little people. Odessa is crying a little bit and humming out loud now. Mama asks her what she's humming. Odessa shakes her head and continues and Mama folds Odessa and me in her arms.

We three breathe together. I hear Pops open the box of cigars on the coffee table and light one up. Once he's puffing away he stops crying and says, This storm has gone through us all and now it's just raining, just big gobs of spit coming our way. Mama still holds us tight. Pops goes out the front door, gently closes it. Mama lets us go and I am all sweaty and then cold as Odessa and Mama pull away from me. Outside, Pops holds his arms to the sky which is brighter now, gray not green, he lets the rain fall on his face, but I can no longer look at him.

30

Nightmare II

Everything is black like the puppies and gold, like Goldie, black and gold. Goldie swirls in the air like a lariat being spun very fast and her arms become whips. I have to stay away from them. The bark on the tree is turning gold. The edges of the grass are turning gold. The Mills sisters sit in their house watching tv when I go to their tree, take an apple from it, to take home to Pops. I find him lying on his bed with his muddy shoes and a puppy in his pocket.

The gold shimmers in the window and I am afraid of it. The puppy starts to moan. The air smells nasty like when Odessa cleans the windows with vinegar and the sun shines through and my nose turns up all on its own. Goldie gets bigger and bigger and the moaning gets louder and louder. The picture explodes. I wake up.

Try and Understand Grownups

Come on Nate, eat your cereal. Sit down and eat, Mama says to Pops who is walking around and around us, unable to do anything but drink his coffee and smoke Mama's cigarettes. Hell's bells, I say, and Mama says, What did you say? I put my head down and look at my chest and try not to watch Pops so much, he's making me dizzy. Pops says, I'm not going back to that office this week, Pops says, I can't stand that old man.

Speak up to him, Mama says in a whispering voice as if Boomer was right in the kitchen.

Do you really think I can tell him what I see in him? He's arrogant and devious. Can I tell him I hate looking at him, how he has horns for ears and a little bookkeeper's mind and how when he walks down the street all the words have a go at him and how much of a cheapskate he is. God Bev. He's awful. Pops' coffee spills out of his cup and it's then that Pops gets annoyed and throws his cigarette into the cup. A nice hiss.

Nate, you know he has only you and your family's best interests at heart.

Pops stops pacing and turns to Mama and says, I hate that frigging man. Pops screams and then he sits down quietly and eats his cereal.

Pops is dressed in his green suit and white shirt and a tie with little ducks on it. I am wearing my sundress with all the buttons up the front and my sandals. Mama is dressed up too because after breakfast, once Pops leaves for work, Mama and I are going shopping.

Nate, Mama says, you're a very accomplished man. You have refinement and good taste. You speak well. People like you. Mama is trying so hard to make him feel good. Maybe if I say I love him too and that he's my Pops, he'll feel better, so I say it, Pops I love you. Pops says, Quiet down little one. Just quiet down. Why? I ask. I'm sitting here too. Mama says, Scags it was nice of you to tell your Pops you love him. She pats my hand.

I finish trying to understand grownups. What sense is there? They don't care what I think. Pops smokes and smokes and now he has a cough and Mama says, I can't keep going through this with you. If you drank less and slept more at night, you'd have a clearer head in the morning.

I think I'll go up to my room, I say, and clear away my bowl and cup of milk and give them to Odessa. She says, Thank you funny face. Up I go, one step then two steps and no one calls me back so I run to my dresser and look at my snails in their green/black water like the color of the sky during a storm. I listen very hard and yes, there's the garage door opening and a motor being turned on, it's from Pops' car. It backs away and is gone.

Mama comes up the stairs to my room. She is wearing her sunglasses in the house and carrying her big white purse. She says, We're going now. Keen-o, I say and put on my blue sunglasses that Pops gave me and off we go.

Once we get into Marshall Fields in Old Orchard, I ask her why she doesn't take her sunglasses off. She runs her hand down my back and says, Don't worry yourself about it. We go to the little girl's section. We look at all the rows and rows of dresses in all different sizes and colors. Hell's bells, I say in a whisper and hold onto Mama's hand. She is staring at a red velvet dress so hard she doesn't hear me.

Scags, Mama says, let's just pick out three dresses to try on. One for school, one for dress and one for play. I don't like to play in dresses, I say and she says, That's okay, you will. Let's try on this velvet one. It's so pretty with the lace bib and little cap sleeves. I think this one will fit you, let me hold it up to you. I stand perfectly still as she says, Don't hunch your shoulders, look at me.

Mama, I ask, why is Pops angry at Boomer? Does

132

Pops really hate Boomer and what did Boomer do? Mama says, Oh you and your questions. Don't worry about Boomer. He can take care of himself. She leads me to the dressing room with an armful of dresses. I don't like any of them, but Mama buys the velvet one for me and says we'll try again when there is more of a selection.

We leave the store and walk to the car. Mama gets behind the wheel and puts her key in the ignition and I look at her long white neck and think she is very pretty and I ask her, Does Pops still love me?

What a silly question, Scags, of course your Pops and I both love you. Do Boomer and Goldie love me? Yes, of course, and Aunt Money. Odessa loves you. You are rich with love.

I know Pops wants to love me, I say, and she says right away, You can be sure of that. We pull out of the parking lot and make a right on Skokie Boulevard. I ask, Do you love me? She says, All mothers love their children. Did your mother love you? I ask. Mama says, No, but that was different. Why? I ask her and now I see she is getting nervous like when you are just about to slip on ice and for only a second more you feel safe before you land on your butt. And it'll hurt. You'll have no one to cry out to because you're all alone. My mother, Mama says, was a very unhappy person. Why? I ask. For a lot of reasons, Mama says and turns onto our street.

We drive past the Mills' house and then the empty

lot and past the Cooks' house and up our drive. We see Pops in the front yard wearing his suit and mowing the lawn. I sit back and wait for Mama to pull into the garage. She stops the car, she has nothing to say, she rests her head on the steering wheel.

Pops keeps mowing the lawn, not looking up at us, chomping on a big cigar and looking mean. Mama slowly leaves the car and says nothing to me. She walks through the kitchen door carrying the green bag with my dress in it and her big white purse and closes the door.

Pops keeps mowing as if he never saw us return. Why isn't he at work downtown with Boomer? Is Mama so unhappy now like her mother was? I leave the car and go to the back yard where the cottonwood tree sits so full and strong and it's cool back here, with a nice breeze. Pops will soon be back here, the grass is very tall. Will he see me then?

Nobody Understands
My Pops But Me

I am in my room on a lazy kind of day where coloring with my crayons, copying the full colors of birds out of my bird book, is just the thing for me. I wonder, of course, because I always wonder, where is that Julia and why hasn't she written to me? I wrote her twice and I asked her all kinds of questions and I want some answers now.

I think of this blue color and this red color and this yellow color and how when they are combined they make other colors and I want Mama and Pops and me to be one big color, like purple.

I hear Mama say, Oh no, in her very worried voice. I hear the voice and I know it has something to do with Pops so I run downstairs and find Mama standing at the picture window in the living room with her fingers on the glass like she told me never to do. I walk up to her and look outside. Pops is running back and forth across the street and setting fires in the neighbors' and our driveways. He has a big red can of gasoline in one hand and a rake in the other and the fires are big and very red. Mama says, Go to your room, Scags.

I run away from her and out the front door, down the hot white cement sidewalk and run run run until I jump and land on Pops' bare back. I can't let anyone hurt him. I can't let him go up in smoke. I hold him around the neck and he laughs and laughs. He puts down the gasoline can and holds onto me. He is all sweaty and the ashes from the fire stick to his chest. He tells me to let go of him and I do. He runs across the street to make the fire higher in the Rappaports' driveway. Mr. Rappaport comes out of his house wearing an angry look. He pulls his hose out of the wheel it is rolled on and turns on the water and the fire tries to stay alive, and Pops stands there watching it die.

What do you think you're doing? Mr. Rappaport asks Pops. Pops says, I'm making a fire and howdy doo to you too, and turns around and returns to our driveway where the blaze is hot and red, yellow, orange. Pops rakes the twigs and newspapers into a tight pile when Mr. Cook comes out of his house and puts out his fire too. Mr. Cook says, Watch out Morgenstern, next time you do something like this, I'll call the cops. I watch Pops. Pops, I say, why a fire?

Someone taps me on my shoulder and I turn around. It's Mr. Arthur. He taps Pops' shoulder and says, Nate this is not a good idea. Pops says, But don't you see if we all burn up in one big blaze how we won't have to live like this, each of us on our own little island and no one to talk to? Pops looks hard at Mr. Arthur. He pulls a handkerchief from his pocket and wipes all the soot and sweat from his face. He is so hot that his glasses are slipping down his nose, and his chin drips.

Mr. Arthur takes the can of gasoline out of Pops' hand and says, Let's go Nate, let's go clean up. He takes the rake and breaks apart the tight little fire and then stomps on it. He and Pops go up the walk to our front door. Mama is standing there on the stoop with Mrs. Arthur and all these eyes are watching Pops who puts his hands to his head. Mr. Arthur puts the can of gasoline on the ground and tells Pops to go inside and take a shower and rest. Mama holds her body to herself as if it might fall apart, and then takes Pops arm. The two of them go inside.

I stand at the foot of the driveway and look at what is left of the deep red glow. I look hard at the ashes to see if some spark is left to ignite it all over again.

Mr. Arthur puts his hand on my shoulder as I stick my white sneaker into the ashes. He has a water can in hand and he begins to pour it over the fire. Please don't, I say, but the water douses what little spirit was left and now it's a mixture of soot and unburned newspapers. It becomes a smoky mess that fills up my eyes with tears which I cannot stop.

After the fire is out I ask Mr. Arthur, Why did Pops do this? He puts the empty can down and spreads out the charred remains with the rake. He stands next to me, rubbing his chin with the rake's handle. Why? Scags. Why? I don't know but sometimes people get ideas in their heads that they just can't keep in control. But now your father has gotten it out of his system and he'll be fine. You'll see.

But everyone is mad at him, I say. Mr. Arthur says, The important people aren't angry at him, just the people who don't understand. You understand, don't you Scags? I nod my head yes, because I should be able to understand. He'll be fine now, Mr. Arthur says again. Since he'll be fine it doesn't have to hurt as much that he has these ideas. Now he's going to be fine, I say to myself as I jump over a crack in the sidewalk and save my mother's back.

Dandelions

Ricky Rappaport is going to let me wear his helmet when we play football tonight after dinner. He found a bunch of guys we could play with and Johnny and Davy and Tony and Sandy and Rebecca are all going to play too. I can't play quarterback, Ricky said, my hands are too small to pass the football, and I can't play center because I wouldn't be able to defend him. But I can run, Ricky said, run fast, faster than anybody on the street. You're right, I said to him, no one beats me in races and when we all run around the block I'm the first one back even though it makes me sick to run that fast and that far. I can catch, too, I said, run, catch and run. I may get tackled so Ricky thought it would be a good thing to wear his helmet.

Odessa is off tonight and Mama cooked what she knows how to cook—steak, corn on the cob, cucumbers and dill in sour cream. My glass of milk seems too tall and the steak is bleeding on the plate and the corn is too hot. If only I could eat fast and not get a stomach ache, but whenever I eat fast, I throw up so I take teeny weeny bites of steak, cutting it into the smallest pieces possible and then I stick the green holders into each end of the corn and butter it really well. I like the crunch of the cucumbers in the sour cream. The idea of playing football I like but I've never played before. I know I can't tell Ricky that. I won't even tell Davy who has shoulder pads and a helmet.

Pops is quiet and dreamy. He's smiling at something funny and Mama tries to get him to share the joke but he pays no attention to her and picks up his ear of corn, quickly biting it like a squirrel. Mama says, Well if no one wants to talk I will and says, Mrs. Arthur and I found a superb little restaurant that sent us coupons in the mail. They had such wonderful crabmeat salads and mint iced tea and I think we should go there sometime for dinner.

Pops lowers his ear of corn and says, I don't like to eat out. I like being home with all my things around me. I don't like to wait for a waiter to take my order which he'll never get right or for him to bring me the check. I like Odessa's cooking fine since I have to pay someone to cook a decent meal.

Mama says, What's wrong with this meal? I thought I cooked the steaks just as you like them and made a light summer fare for us.

Okay, Bev, Pops says, if that's what you think you did, I won't argue with you.

Pops, I say, didn't you like the dinner? I loved

it. Then I say, I'm going to play football now. I have cleaned my plate and now I'm going outside to play.

Pops looks at me and then turns to Mama and says, This is all your fault. You don't know how to raise a girl.

The next thing I know, Pops jumps out of his chair and grabs my arm so hard it hurts and he says to me, You're going to pick dandelions. I am so surprised. Pops never did this before. Pops drags me to the garage, but if he let go of my arm I would follow him even though I don't want to. He pulls the weeder off his work bench and hands it to me. It looks like a little hand with the fingers making a v. He is still holding my arm and takes me to the back yard. He says, Pick all the dandelions and don't chop their heads off, go down to the roots and kill them, I want this yard yellow-free tonight.

Mama is standing at the back door watching us and I feel this hot liquid in my throat. Won't she do anything? There are thousands of dandelions on the lawn and I bend over to pull one out and Pops says, get on your knees, you'll do a better job. Tears stream out of my eyes and snot builds up in my nose. Pops says, We'll have none of that now, work steadily and you'll get it done. You know how it is with dandelions, you've got to get them when they're young.

I can't pick all of them tonight, I say, with my throat tightening up so that I can't breathe. Pops stands over me.

Mama comes outside and stands next to Pops. She bends down to me and takes the weeder out of my hand and says, Go play Scags, stay outside until it gets dark. She takes the weeder out of my hands, I feel her cool hand over mine. I run out of our yard. I hear her say to me that Pops doesn't feel well. But I keep running as fast as I can and as far as I can while Pops starts to yell, Scaags, Scaaaags, please.

I don't play football but keep running all the way down the street until I'm at the foot of the hill leading to Witch's Well.

In what light there is, I climb the hill and sit with my body all collapsed onto me, grabbing my ankles, tightening my knees and I know, yes, I know, he's not fair anymore. But it's not fair not fair to make me miss the game and leave me out here. It is getting dark. The frogs and crickets kick up a storm of noise, a veritable symphony, as Pops would say. Yes. I listen and wait for the spooks but it's a long wait and nothing happens. I get up and brush the dirt off my butt and start the walk home. I see them standing at the picture window, looking for me. Pops with his arm around Mama and Mama resting her head on his shoulder. They're waiting for me. I think for the very first time in my life I don't want to go home.

Nightmare III

The dandelions are so high as an elephant's eye and I dig and dig. Little worms I chop in twos, threes, fours. I have a big rock in my throat that is so heavy I am afraid I will sink through the ground so fast that I will be in the center of the earth with no way back up. I try to stand up. I try to be stronger than the rock but as I push myself up, push, push, this weight this rock is so big and it is stuck in my throat. I can't swallow it or cough it up. I get to my feet but I know I will never be without this rock and it is caught in my throat so deep that I cannot scream as the worms crawl up my legs. I try to crush them but there are more and more. I must scream. I must. But I can't.

35

Scags with a Black Eye

It doesn't take much to get into a fight in my neighborhood. Davy is in them all the time because kids are always making fun of his mother. The gypsy, they call her and even worse. I just watch and when they're on the ground I run home and tell Odessa so she can stop it. But she says, Oh never mind, they'll be the best buddies tomorrow. So when Davy says to me that Ricky's been saying things about my Pops, I march straight over to Ricky's house with Davy close behind.

I knock on the door and when his little brother Bobby answers I say, Tell your brother to stop saying things about my Pops. Ricky hears me and comes to the door. You're scared of me, I say. He says, Your old man is a crazy and everyone knows it. He says this all through the screen door like he doesn't want to fight me and that makes him look like a skinny little nothing and I tell him to come outside and say that to me.

Davy says, Scags don't start a fight. He pulls on

144

my arm and says, Let's go home, we can play in my mother's bedroom. I yell at him, Go away, you little homo. For sure he gets angry at me and hauls his arm back and bops me right in the eye. I fall down more because he surprised me than because he hurt me. Ricky's laughing and Bobby is too. Davy takes off faster than I have ever seen him run. I hear Davy screaming, Your dad's a loony and you are too. I sit on that front lawn so long that Ricky and Bobby go inside leaving me there with an already shut eye.

I go home. I take my time because my butt hurts and so does my face. I touch my eyelid and already it is hot and puffy. I wonder how I am going to hide this shiner from everyone. Davy shouldn't have hit me when he knew I really wanted to fight Ricky. I don't want them all to think that Pops is crazy.

I go into my back yard to my tree and sit down. My eye hurts so bad and I know, I know, no one is going to not notice my eye and what do I say to Pops when he sees right through me. He'll know I'm more hurt than Davy's punch. My eye is swollen shut and even lying down on the grass doesn't make it better. I get up and walk to the back door. Odessa is at the sink, looks up at me, and her eyes become as big as stars and out of her mouth comes a trail of Oh my Gods, so that I think she is never going to be quiet.

I put my finger to my lips. It doesn't work. Mama has heard her and comes running. She takes one look at me and bursts out saying, How did this happen?

Who hit you? I start crying. I can't help it. Mama says, Shush, shush now.

Odessa says, Those children got nothing better to do but beat up little girls? Mama bends down to take a look, a close look at my eye. Odessa takes a cold rag and sets it on my face. What happened to you? Odessa asks, who hit you? I can't stop crying. The cold aches my head. My butt hurts. As I cry some more, Mama holds me, and I say to myself for as long as Mama holds me, I'll cry. Mama runs her hand through my hair and I cry even harder for my long lost hair, and for the way everyone says Pops, my Pops, is crazy and I want to know what is happening to him.

Mama picks me up and carries me through the kitchen, up the stairs to my room. She says, You're getting to be a big girl. I rest my head on her shoulder and wish we could walk like this forever.

When we get to my room she lowers me to the bed and I wrap my arms around her neck and don't let go. What is it Scags? Mama asks in my ear. What happened? I whisper in her ear, Everyone says bad things about Pops. Everyone says he's crazy. My tears wet Mama's face, I think, until I hear her crying too. She pushes me to the side of the bed and lies down next to me, her face in my neck and her arm thrown across my stomach.

Mama says, We're still his favorite girls, you know, and he's trying the best he can and he is still your Pops. I say, But all these things he does, like setting fires you know and the dandelions—Shush, shush now, Mama says and puts her finger over my lips. It smells like perfume, her perfume, the one she wears every day and that settles on all of us. I kiss her finger and she taps my lips a couple of times.

Mama says, Don't get in anymore fights. They don't understand how it is with Pops. Okay? You promise? she asks and tickles my stomach. When I laugh and wrinkle up my nose it hurts. My whole head hurts and I yell stop. Mama stops.

I'm sorry, she says, that your friends don't understand, but you do, don't you, your Pops is going through a bad time. A very bad time and we need to be strong and love him and believe that he'll get better soon.

Do you love me, Mama? I ask. What a silly question to ask, Mama says, and then she sits up next to me, puts the cold towel over both my eyes and says in a very soft voice, as if she were telling a secret, Of course I do. She gets up and leaves my room. I hear her close the door and walk downstairs.

Dancing

Did you ever see your parents dance, did you? I ask Odessa in the morning. She says, My parents danced all the time when they weren't hoeing, chopping, plowing, picking, making money anyway they knew how. Dancing, we had plenty of dancing with ten kids to raise and feed and clothe. Dancing? Let me tell you about dancing.

Odessa tells me a story about how she and her husband met at a dance club on the South Side. Odessa wore yellow heels and a grape purple dress and a yellow turban. She looked so beautiful. She met a man who loved to dance with her to show up all the other couples there. They danced all night and did that every Saturday night for three months before he asked her out on a real date. He was a fine dancer, she says, a handsome man next to a woman. Hah! Odessa says, You saw your parents dancing? When? she asks. I say, Last night. Ah, Odessa says, That living room smelled like perfume and champagne. They cleaned up everything. What do you know about that?

They danced in the living room to records. They thought I was sleeping but I heard them in my sleep, they woke me up and I could smell them and when I peeked at them I saw they were all dressed up but only went to the living room.

Mama wore this beautiful dress that danced as good as her and Pops wore a black suit with a white shirt and a red bow tie. There were candles everywhere and they had a bottle of champagne and some food out and they were like a bride and groom.

When Pops took Mama in his arms she smiled at him so nice, so pretty, with her white teeth and dimples and the funny way she lifts her head to the side when something nice happens. I watched for only a little while. Actually, a long time because they were so graceful and they danced so perfectly around the room, never bumping into anything or stepping on each other's toes. Mama wore such high high heels that she was almost as tall as Pops. They got romantic with each other, mushy. I liked the music. Mama's dress shimmered in the candlelight and Pops' black hair looked lighter. They didn't look like parents. I went back to bed.

Hush little one, Odessa says, and down the stairs come Mama and Pops. They look dreamy and happy and Odessa and I watch them.

I stare at Pops first. He is trying not to giggle, to laugh out loud at how happy he is. I can see in his eyes, well, I guess I shouldn't look him in the eyes because they are a little scary. I look at his mouth where I see his berry-red lips. I look at his hands. Are they shaking? No. He isn't dancing but he did dance all last night. And Mama? She looks sleepy. Her hair is going in so many directions that she could scare an octopus.

Pops says, Scags we're going to have to get a steak for that eye. A raw slab of a side of cow and cover up that shiner that isn't even worth crying about. I stare at my hands. I walk over to Odessa standing by the counter, putting cereal in a bowl for Pops. I wrap my arms around her, and she whispers, It's okay. Once he eats, he'll be fine.

Why are we all standing around as if someone died, Pops asks. He pulls a cigarette from behind his ear, lights it and walks to his spot. Odessa, Odessa, he says, I need . . . I need . . . She says, A bowl of cereal? She unwraps me and walks to the table with his cereal and a cup of coffee oh so white. She sets them down in front of him and Pops says, No, not that. Then he says no more but stares at his cigarette. The ash gets longer and longer. I know I should get him an ashtray. I know I should move toward him and catch that ash, but it's too late and it falls onto the blue linen placemat. Mama goes toward Pops and sits down in my place, and drinks my milk.

Nate, Mama says, looking at him. I look too. He seems frozen in place. Mama reaches for his left hand, the hand holding the cigarette. It is still burning and could burn his fingers because he's not paying any attention to it. Mama pries Pops' fingers open and takes the cigarette from him. Odessa brings an ashtray that is wet and Mama drops the butt into it where the flame makes a hissing sound like kisses as it goes out.

Pops jumps up from his chair so suddenly that it falls backwards behind him. He takes a step and stops. He takes another step and stops. The three of us watch him. I don't know what to do so I run out of the kitchen, up the stairs to my bedroom and slam the door behind me.

What is happening to my Pops? Why doesn't someone do something, I say. Do something to make him stop being so scary and put him back the way he was when he would come home from work and pick me up and let me walk in the air and twirl me around saying my name over and over, Scags, Scaaags, my Scags, and I would say, Yes, you are my Pops.

The Fight

It's early in the morning. I hear loud voices. I hear Mama and Pops yelling. I open my eyes and around the shade I see some light but not much. Pops must have had another one of his nights. I try to hear what Mama is saying to Pops. Pops yells something back at her. Boom boom. Mama comes up the stairs and goes to their bedroom and slams the door. Pops follows close behind her saying, So you think you can do better, you think there are other guys out there as good as me, you think you can just leave us and not pay for it? She screams back, Go to hell. I hear her crying.

She runs out of the room and down the stairs. The garage door opens. She starts her car and pulls out of the driveway. Then I hear nothing. Pops doesn't do anything. I have to get out of bed.

Pops stands in the hallway, his hands covering his face. He didn't do anything to keep Mama at home. I grab him by the belt and say, What's wrong Pops, why are you crying, where did Mama go?

He puts his arms down and rests one hand on my shoulder. He stops crying immediately. Pops says, Well I guess it's just the two of us, kiddo. When is Mama coming back, I ask Pops, where did she go? Why did she leave? Pops asks, Do you know how to make coffee?

I say, No. I look at him. He needs to shave and put cold water on his eyes. He needs me, I think suddenly, I think maybe I can fix him. Or maybe this is a dream and I'll wake up soon. I say, You know Pops we could have some coffee together and then we could play with my microscope. He says, Yes, that is true.

Scags, Scags, Scags, he says my name over and over as if he didn't know I was standing right next to him. We go down to the kitchen in the dark. He seems calm now as if he doesn't remember all the screaming. Yes, Pops is going to be okay now.

The phone rings. He doesn't answer it. I go to pick it up, and he says, No don't, let it ring. I say, It could be Mama. He says, Yes. I say, Mama needs to be here. Pops rubs his face with the back of his hand. I like that and I do it too. My face doesn't make a noise like a woolen sweater all full of electricity because I don't have a beard. I look at Pops and then at me. We're standing exactly the same way, one leg crossed in front of the other. We both like our coffee with lots of milk.

I say, Pops, make some coffee for the three of us. He says, Okay and pulls the pot off the counter and measures out the grounds and the water and puts it on the stove. Now I know Mama will come home soon and I can go back to bed. The phone rings again. It rings for a long time and then stops. Pops walks to the phone and takes it off the hook and we wait for the coffee, holding hands and wiping the tears from our eyes.

We wait a long time for the coffee and when Pops pours it into my cup it is so black it looks like asphalt. He puts the pot back on the stove and then goes to the refrigerator and takes out the milk and pours lots of it into his cup and then mine. He sets the bottle down on the counter and I have to say, Pops, put the milk away. I say, Pops I like my coffee just the way you do. He says, But of course, and puts a big spoonful of sugar in mine, stirs it up and I can see that he is trying to smile and we both wipe the last of the tears from our eyes. He says, Careful now, as I walk to the table with my coffee.

I sit down and sip little sips of coffee. Pops says, Like your coffee that way do you Scags? He comes to the table and sits in Mama's place and runs his finger around the rim of the cup. The coffee is warm and sweet. I keep thinking I'll hear Mama in the garage soon. He says, If this were a wine glass I could make music. I tell him, Go get a wine glass, go ahead Pops, get a wine glass and make music. He jumps from the table , knocking the edge of it and my coffee sways back and forth looking like melted ice cream.

Pops goes into the dining room where the wine glasses are kept and opens the buffet and pulls out a blue glass with a very thin rim. I follow Pops around as he holds the glass up and then goes back to the kitchen. At the sink he fills the glass with water almost to the top. He takes a sip of the water and then a bigger sip and then empties the glass and sets it in the dish drainer.

Hey Pops, I say what about making music? Making music, he says, and bends down and says, Stand on my shoes. I like this game, I say, but what about the glass? He says, Penny ante stuff, this is the big time. Hold onto me. I wrap my arm around his waist and he begins to hum when the red red robin comes bob bob bobbing along, tapping on my head and dancing, dancing, dancing, as if we were taking giant steps in the snow. We are dancing no matter how tired we are. If only my Pops could be this way all the time, happy, and singing and dancing I would never again ask for a puppy and I would keep my room neat and eat all my peas and as soon as I say this to myself—no puppies, make bed, eat peas—I hear him laughing, laughing, laughing and the room begins to spin and he picks me up and twirls me around and around like a rope, I start to giggle but then I get scared. I am frightened that he is going to swing me so fast that I'll turn into butter and will turn into a spot on the floor for Odessa to clean up.

Pops, I say, sort of crying, please stop. He's laughing and laughing and then he stops suddenly both the twirling and the laughing and sets me down. I fall to my knees on the floor. Pops walks away. I am dizzy but I get up and follow him. There is some light in the living room where he has gone. I have to touch the wall to walk without falling down. It seems like a long walk from the kitchen to the living room.

He sits in his chair and lights up a cigar. The living room is kind of dark, but I see Mama's cigarettes on the table next to the couch. I light one and sit there in the dark with Pops, choking but smoking.

Mama comes home to find me and Pops sitting there, smoke filling the air. She says, Nate, are you crazy letting her smoke? What do you think you're doing? Scags, she says, Give me that cigarette. I get off the couch and hand it to her and she immediately takes a puff.

The front door opens again and there is Aunt Money looking like she's been up for hours too and could use some coffee. But before I can offer her any, Aunt Money comes over to me and says, Honey, let's go upstairs and let your folks talk. She takes my hand and we go up the stairs to my bedroom where she tells me to lie down, she covers me up, and we turn on the radio and listen to the morning news.

Over the radio I hear shouting, it's Mama and then the silence of Pops. I say to Aunt Money, Why did Mama leave me? Is she going to stay home now?

Aunt Money says, Yes, she will. I say, She is so angry at my Pops that maybe she'll leave us. Aunt Money sits straight up on the bed next to me and looks me right in the eye and says, I think your Mama and Pops want to live with you, all three of you together.

It gets quiet. Mama comes upstairs. She stands in the doorway and asks Aunt Money if she would mind taking me home with her for the day while she and Pops try to iron things out. No one asks me anything. Aunt Money says, Yes, that would be nice to spend the day together, just the two of us girls. Where is Pops and what is he doing? I ask Mama. But she turns her face to me, says nothing, and I can see how tired she is and that she has been crying too. Mama? I ask, and she says, Scags, we'll talk later, just go into the city with Aunt money and have some fun.

I get out of my bed and open the dresser drawer where my underwear is and put on clean underpants and an undershirt. Mama silently goes to the closet and pulls out my pink shirt and shorts and I get dressed. Mama says, Don't forget to brush your teeth and comb your hair. When I come back from the bathroom, Aunt Money helps me buckle my shoes and then we go downstairs and out the front door.

It is light now and the grass is all wet. Aunt Money's blue Buick sits in the driveway, her windshield is all wet too. I climb in the back seat and Aunt Money pulls out of the driveway into the street. The drapes are closed in the living room and everyone on the block is asleep.

Makeup

Aunt Money drives fast, like Pops, and as we drive downtown to her apartment the Lake is so shiny and speckled in the early morning light. I ask Aunt Money did Boomer and Goldie ever act like my Pops and Mama? I ask her that as we turn onto her street and she looks for a parking space. She says nothing until we are parked and entering her apartment. Then she says, Grownups fight but then it's over and they makeup. When she turns the key in the lock she looks at me, she seems so much taller than me and I'm hanging onto her skirt and the door opens and I smell Mama everywhere.

You know, Scags, everyone starts out with a pretty decent sort of parents, your Mama and Pops are just having some problems they need to fix, Aunt Money says as I wander around the room taking in Mama's smell. Mama was here, I say, and I see all the glasses and ashtrays sitting around as if there had been a party. Her green couch has three sections and I lie down on the first one and see that I only reach from head to foot the first section. I ask again, Did this ever happen to you?

Yes, Aunt Money says, as she goes around the room, picking up the glasses and ashtrays and going into her tiny kitchen and then she comes to me on the couch with a big glass of orange juice. These things happen all the time, Aunt Money says.

Mama was here a long time, I say, as she hands me the juice. I say, I can't drink all of this, and she says, I'll share it with you. Are you hungry? Yes, I say. Would you like some toast with your juice? she asks me and I get up and go to her little dining room table and sit down like Mama would tell me to do. The chairs are big and heavy and have the same seat covers as the couch. I sit up very straight and fold my hands in my lap and say to Aunt Money, I like my toast to have lots of butter on it. She walks by me, tickles the top of my head, and goes into the kitchen. She says, It's amazing how much of your hair has grown back already. I know she is just saying that to cheer me up. But Aunt Money, I ask, what if Mama is still angry at Pops for cutting it?

Oh, oh, oh, I see what you mean, Aunt Money says as she puts the toast in the toaster. Her kitchen is all white except for the floor which is black. When you stand at the stove and do nothing more than turn around you are at the sink. Aunt Money says, Hair grows back. Don't worry. She opens her refrigerator and says, If you want eggs, no can do, but you could have some liverwurst on your toast.

For breakfast, I ask, don't you have any cereal and bananas? She looks at me and says, No, no cereal, no bananas, there probably isn't any milk but I do have a soup or two.

Gosh, Aunt Money, I say, what do you eat for breakfast? Aunt Money shakes her head and says, Well I don't really eat breakfast and when I do whatever happens to be here. So how about some soup? Okay, I say, and connect the dots of red stains on the white table cloth with my finger.

Aunt Money, I say, why don't Boomer and Goldie fix things up? Aunt Money lets out a loud howl, long and free as if her girdle snapped open. What a question, she says, what a little observer you are, she says. Maybe when you're older you'll be able to understand that sometimes adults get into messes they don't quite know how to clean up. It just takes time, she says, as she hands me my toast all crisp and buttery. I eat it quickly because I am hungry and I do want to be here with Aunt Money. I do.

Aunt Money sits down at the table with me and picks up my toast and starts to eat it. Hey, I say, why can't you make some toast for yourself? I don't have anymore bread, Aunt Money says. I'll just heat up your soup and then we can try to disguise that shiner. I put my finger on my eyelid. It feels soft and sore and puckered as if a raisin was in there.

Aunt Money puts my soup in a bowl. It is hot and steamy. I am going to pretend it's oatmeal in the winter time, that it's cold outside and I need something warm in me to fortify myself, as Odessa says.

Aunt Money sits at the table with me. I put my spoon in the white bowl and stir the pieces of chicken, letting the steam rise up in my face. Would you like to have me put some makeup on your eye Scags? We've got the whole day together and it would be nice to try and hide that big black eye. I could polish your nails. We could go shopping and find you a pretty dress with a big bow in the back and a pair of little patent leather shoes. What do you say? I think of sitting at her dressing table where all her potions and powders and magic wands are lined up in rows, level upon level in so many fancy cases but I really don't want to put any of that stuff on my face.

I start to cry, I don't know why. Aunt Money pulls a tissue out of a big pocket and comes over to me and wipes my tears away and puts the tissue under my nose and says, Blow, blow harder. I can't stop. She pulls my chair away from the table and picks me up and takes me into her bedroom where her enormous bed with the canopy over it sits in the center. She puts me down and takes off my sandals and pulls an afghan off the chair next to the bed and throws it over me. It is grey and blue and she once told me that Goldie and she took turns working on it when Aunt Money was a little girl. It settles down on me and it feels good, like a weight to keep me from floating into space.

I say, Aunt Money, don't go. She says, I'm not going anywhere. I guess we're both tired and I'll lie down with you. Sleep now, sleep will make everything better and you'll see that your Mama and Pops are going to be fine. You will be fine too and there's a whole lifetime ahead for dressing up, makeup, and it can wait.

I push myself next to her, I hold her arm and I think of Pops twirling me in the air and Mama looking so sad and Aunt Money starts to snore. I close my eyes, and I am dizzy, I am small, and I need to pee. But I don't want to get up. I don't want to move away from Aunt Money. But I really have to pee. So I get up quietly and put the blanket back over Aunt Money and go to the bathroom.

I sit down on the toilet with the door closed, staring at myself in the mirror on the back of the bathroom door. I wonder what are Mama and Pops doing now? I could be in my own bed. I look hard at myself and don't want to leave the bathroom. My red hair is going in every direction and as I stand up I see my bony knees and long arms. I look at my face and pucker up my lips and kiss myself and say everything is going to be keen-o in a minute, no an hour, and then Aunt Money and I can go to my house and we'll eat real food and have a good time. Double keen-o. No funny money honey, I say to the mirror me and smile at me and go back to Aunt Money's bed. I fall asleep without even thinking that this is what I should do.

Pops' Closet

I can hear most of what Boomer, Goldie, Aunt Money and Mama are saying as I lie on Mama's bed. But I can't hear Pops. I don't know what he is trying to tell them all, trying to say, I guess, that everything will be all right now. He'll be fine. No more fights. No more bowling at home. No more fires. And what didn't I think of? How could I have forgotten, no more staying home. Pops will go back to work with a brand new attitude, that's what Boomer says.

Their bed is not made. Odessa must be letting it air out. The sheets feel like satin and are so smooth that I feel like I could float away if I close my eyes. I'm not allowed in the living room with all the grownups. And since I am the only child, I have to entertain myself. Someone is crying. Is it Pops? No, it's me. I hear myself crying from a long ways away. Like a train in the distance before the gates go down. Pops too I think. Pops is probably crying because things have been so bad for so long now. So he'll be fixed. So so so.

Maybe I can fix Pops. I get off their bed and go to Mama's dressing table and sit down. It hurts to look in the mirror. I'm not at all myself, as Mama would say. I am all a fright, she would say. How can I fix myself, she would say.

Here it is Friday afternoon. All my family is downstairs where I can't go. When I look at myself, it hurts. When I think of Pops I want to run downstairs and hold onto him tight and we can do anything he wants like go to his office and he'll show Boomer how he swings me around and how we love to dance together and my hair is red, not black like Pops' and Mama's hair. Mine is red, red, red, like the tip of a lit cigar, like the tip of my Pops' lit cigar. I know my Pops could never go anywhere without his so white coffee and long, long cigars. He couldn't go anywhere without me because I won't let him.

Maybe Pops needs to be reminded of how he used to be. Maybe he forgot. Keen-o. I know what to do. I look all over Mama's table for something black, a black cream, but of course she doesn't have any. Why do I need black cream? I think about that and go to Pops' closet. I open the door. On the floor is his green jacket and yellow-and-green tie. The jacket is all wrinkled and dirty, as if Pops slept outside. It feels heavy like it wants to stay on the floor.

I pick it up and search in his pockets. I pull out my rocks, the rocks from my collection. What are they doing in Pops' pocket? Why did Pops steal my rocks?

Shouldn't Pops have asked me if he could have them? Why does Pops want them? I put them on the floor, there's the one that Davy gave me, the one with the shiny layer of mica in the middle. Here's my fool's gold rock that I know isn't really gold but I told myself it is, that it can buy me all the candy I could possibly want. I pick up the rocks and put them in Pops' shoe and next to his shoes is the black cream I was looking for.

I open it and it smells strong, like leather and sweat, it is almost gone but there is a liitle bit left on the sides of the round can. I stick me fingers into it, the fingers of both hands and rub the goopy cream into my hair. It gets weighted down and held in place like Pops' hair. I put as much in my hair as there is in the can. Then I put on Pops' jacket, pull his loafers out of the closet and look for his glasses. His black glasses. Where are they? Why can't I find them? They've got to be here. Yes. Here they are under the bed. Why are they there?

I pick up his glasses and put them on. I can't see a thing. I look at myself in the mirror with Pops' glasses on, with Pops' jacket on, his shoes and his black hair. I can't see a thing as I go down the stairs, slow, one step at a time, because everything is too big and I'm too little but I know when Pops sees me he'll remember how he used to be and get up from his chair and pick me up and swirl me around and I will walk on the ceiling again which I haven't done in the longest time and I make it down the stairs.

I walk to the living room and no one is talking so I throw myself in front of them with a big ta da. Mama screams. Celia Harper Morgenstern—but Pops doesn't even turn to look at me. I want to sit in Pops' lap but everyone is yelling, except Pops. Mama keeps saying, Don't touch anything, Pops sits in his robe staring down at something. Odessa appears and takes a look at me and says, Aw child, what have you done? She takes me up in her arms and I grab her neck. I wrap my arms around her neck. Pops' shoes fall off my feet.

Pops, I say, Pops, look at me, as Odessa carries me out of the room and he turns around in his chair and I hear Goldie say, Odessa get her cleaned up, and Aunt Money say, What have you done and Boomer say, Oh God what is wrong with that child? But Pops' face is strange. He's smiling, he's laughing, but not at me.

40

Julia Is Home

I'm in my bedroom where Mama told me to go after breakfast. I'm being punished for making my hair black and getting polish all over the walls. It took Odessa all evening to wash it out of my hair. You are really too much today, Mama said to me. I started laughing when she said that, as I drank my orange juice. It flew out of my glass and all over the table. Mama told me to clean up the mess I made because Odessa had enough to do cleaning up after me. I turned to Pops. He hadn't shaved again or put on his glasses. He drank his coffee black and said nothing while Mama was telling me what a bad girl I was. He didn't say anything or look at me or say my name. No.

Odessa rinsed out a dish cloth and handed it to me. It was hot and I had to juggle it back and forth from one hand to the other. I tried to get all the sticky juice off the table. I washed off every plate while everyone watched me. I tried to get it all up, but it had gone everywhere. I sang a little tune and did a little soft shoe as I went around the table trying to clean it up.

Odessa said, Scags, why don't you let me finish what you started, you're making a mess of the glass. No, I said very loud. Pops flinched. I scrubbed the table clean and then Mama told me to go to my room.

Why is everyone so quiet, why isn't Pops singing or whistling? Why do I have to go to my room? I'd rather go outside and ride my bike, I said to Mama. I'm saying to you, Mama said, go to your room now.

I saluted her, turned toward Odessa who was rinsing out the dish cloth and she said, What are you looking at me for, you heard your mother. Okay, I said to them all, even Pops who was staring out the window and not paying attention to me. Okay. I'm going. Do you read me? Over and out. I saw my feet as two big cabooses, so heavy and tired I could barely lift them up the stairs. I called to them, I'm going. No one said anything. I'm at the top of the stairs, I said. Mama said, Go to your room and close the door. I made my caboose shoes slide slowly and slowly and when I got to my room, I slammed the door.

The sun is coming into my room like swords being drawn for a fight. One sword smashes my pillows. One sword sits hot and heavy on the foot of my bed. I walk to the windows for a little breeze and so I don't have to think about Mama being angry with me and Pops not even seeing me. I look at my tree. It is so tall and it can't possibly fall down. Oh, I say, turning my head, there's Davy and his mother in their back yard.

She's talking to him, her hair is blonde and sparkles in the sun. Davy is kicking at the ground with the toe of his shoe, dust rising and spinning, grey and white and I say, Davy, hey Davy. He doesn't hear me. I call again. His mother hears me and takes Davy's hand and leads him inside. I want to go for a ride with Davy and tell him it's okay now about my shiner. Surely we could play cowboys and Indians. I walk away from the window to get my gun with caps in it. I want to shoot Davy even though I'm not allowed to shoot the caps inside. I take three giant steps to the chair at my desk and hanging from it is my holster and gun. I pick it up and put it around my waist and belt it. I go back to the window.

I hear someone calling my name. I hear it like a baseball fitting into a mitt. I hear it and I know it is Julia. I turn my head and there she is in her back yard, standing on the patio chair, her arms running in circles, her long arms and legs, her face smiling and laughing and happy. I put my palm on the screen as if I could magically reach through it.

Come on, Julia says. Come here, I'm home. I say to myself this is a special occasion, this is reason to sneak out of the house. I unbuckle my holster and let it fall on the floor and yell quietly, I'll be right there.

I leave my room on tip toe. On tip toe I walk out of my room and close the door, down the stairs, and I think oh keen-o I'll get a cigar for us. Pops won't miss one of his schimmelpfennigs, oh hey, I take two out of the wooden box on the coffee table, put them in my back pocket, I leave the house by the front door.

Jumping the hedge between Julia's house and mine, I run run run to her. Julia is jumping all over the patio and when she sees me she stops jumping and looks at me funny. What? I ask her. She puts her finger to my eye, my black eye. Julia asks me what happened. I got into a fight. What for? She asks, and why do you fight? Did it hurt? Only a little bit, a tiniest hurt. Now it itches. And your hair, Scags, why did you cut your hair? I didn't cut it. Pops cut it. Why? Julia asks and I say he couldn't help it. He got confused.

I don't understand, Julia says. I say, It's okay, Odessa fixed it.

Who hit you? Julia asks again. I say right away, No one you know. Do you want to smoke a cigar? Who don't I know Scags? Julia asks but as I pull the two little cigars out of my pocket, Julia stops asking the questions. She laughs and jumps around again and I put my fingers to my lips, Shush Julia. Please. Not so loud and she whispers, Lets go inside. My mother is sleeping. What about your father? I ask and she says, I don't know, we'll see.

We leave the patio and walk toward her back door as if we had nothing special on our minds. Nothing special at all. No we're just going inside for a few minutes, a little rest from the sun.

We go in the back door, through the kitchen where Mrs. Arthur's big black purse sits on the table and Julia steals a book of matches from there and we walk down the hall. Mr. Arthur is in his bathroom with the door open. He doesn't see us because he's got a little scissor up his nose and he's cutting the hairs. We try not to stare or giggle. He doesn't see us and Julia sticks her fist in her mouth to keep quiet. We take giant steps to the bathroom down the hall that she shares with her mother.

Julia grabs my arm and pulls me into the bathroom and closes the door quietly. We stand in the dark. We each have a cigar and we clench them between our teeth. I turn on the light over the sink and we sit down on the edge of the tub. It is hard and cold.

Julia asks, Do you really want to smoke this? She says, Lets pretend. She pretends to smoke it and to blow smoke like a big kid and she says, Look at my smoke rings. I take the matches from her and light one. I put it up to the tip of her cigar. She takes a puff and lets the smoke sit in her mouth. I light the tip of mine and try to inhale and I almost throw up. I start to choke because it is so hot and I start to cough and I can't stop. Julia jumps up and down telling me to please keep quiet. Of course, I can't. I'm choking to death.

There is a knock on the door. That shuts me up. We run the cigars under water and throw them in the garbage. The door opens. There is Mr. Arthur. He looks at Julia and then at me. He fills up the doorway.

What's going on in here? Julia, he says, looking

straight at her with big eyes as if he doesn't really want to know what's going on but he must because he is the father. Julia says, We weren't doing anything. Scags, Mr. Arthur says, Do you want to tell me what you were doing in here? It smells like someone's been smoking. I don't want to make anyone else mad at me, so I say, We were just practicing but we won't do it anymore, I promise, I say. Julia promises too.

Mr. Arthur looks a little angry now and he tells Julia she is grounded for the rest of the day. And you Scags, I won't tell anyone in your house what went on here but I expect you to. So run along now. Julia go to your room.

I walk back down the hallway and out their front door and around the corner and up the front walk. I know Mr. Arthur is angry at me, and I don't like that, but maybe if I just tell Odessa nothing worse will happen today.

As I walk toward the door, Julia jumps out of the bushes and scares me. She climbed out of her bedroom window. She wants to be with me. As the clouds punch out the sun and the breeze turns wilder, all I want to do is sit with Julia under my tree and listen, look, see and smell the new storm coming up. Julia skips along at my side. We go quickly into the back yard and sit down over Lizzie's grave and we hold hands. Julia is here. Julia is home.

Bookmobile II

Every day now, it's Mama saying, Scags do this or Celia do that. She is making me mad. She is mad at Pops, too, always telling him to stop staring at her, to eat his dinner and to stop drinking and bowling. First he looks at her like what are you talking about and then he laughs, laughs so funny, like he's laughing at something neither Mama nor I can see. He laughs. Mama gets up from the table and yells at Odessa that there are water spots on the glasses. Odessa doesn't say anything but I know she knows Mama doesn't mean it.

It is only two weeks before school starts again. Oh no. I got the letter in the mail telling me what teacher I'm going to have and what room number. I'm going to have Mrs. Showalter. Mrs. Showalter's father was a friend of Boomer's. Maybe she'll like me best because of that.

With the teeny clouds running all over the blue sky, it feels kind of cool today. Under the tree is even a cooler place to sit and in my shorts and t-shirt I see little bumps on my skin, on my arms, which are covered with freckles and on my legs. I don't think Mama will let me ride today on Julia's new tandem bicycle. Mr. Arthur bought Julia this keen-o bike and she said we could take a long ride today, maybe all the way to Church Street and Crawford, the furthest away I'm allowed to go on my own. There is a lot of busy traffic there. It's not so easy to cross. I need a grownup to go with me.

Julia says, Scags. I look up and across the yard and she is standing in her mother's flower bed. I see her with her long blonde hair tied up on her head like a ballerina. She pretends to be smoking a cigarette but it's a candy cane, and I say, Can I have one too? You have to come with me to the bookmobile if you want one, she says.

I stand up and wipe the dirt off the back of my shorts. I walk to my front yard and Julia walks in the same direction. Through the bushes she hands me a red and white candy cane. I stick it in my mouth and at first it makes my eyes tear but then I like the sticky sweetness of it. As I pass by the front door, there is Pops holding it open, whistling, leaning against the door and whistling nothing I've ever heard before and sort of like someone who doesn't know how to whistle trying to whistle.

Hi Pops, I say, but he is looking at his shoes, not at me. He's wearing his shiny black shoes and his green suit with a white shirt and the green and yellow tie. He reaches into his jacket pocket and pulls out a rock, one of my rocks, and hands it to me. It's the one with fool's gold in it and it glows. I say, Keep it Pops. I can get more. He tosses it in the air, pulls it to him and replaces it in his pocket. Thanks, he says.

Julia says, Come on Scags, lets go. Pops turns his head in the direction of Julia's voice but when he looks at her and after she says, Hi Mr. Morgenstern, he says to me, Well got to cook the bacon, and he opens the door and walks back into the house.

What's wrong with your dad? Julia asks me in my ear as we walk down the lawn to the bookmobile. Oh, he's just tired, I say, I say, maybe I should get him a book to read. What will you get him? Julia asks. He doesn't look like he's in the mood to read.

What do you mean? I ask Julia. He's fine. People who are tired like to get into bed with a good book.

Yes Scags, he'll be fine soon, Julia says as we climb up the two little steps into the bookmobile where the old lady sits, reading at her table, not even looking up when we come in, I say, He's just got a lot on his mind. Then I say, Hi bookmobile lady, we're here.

She looks up at us and says, Edna, my name is Edna. Your names are Julia and Celia.

No, I say, she's Julia and I'm Scags. Just plain old Scags.

Scags is it, well then Scags, what book would you like today? I don't know, I say, not something sad like

Old Yeller. Maybe I could read Heidi again.

Scags, you've read it a million times, Julia says, so I say, Well then I'll read it a million more times until I have it memorized.

Would you like to live with your grandfather? Julia asks me and I say, Boomer's okay. But not to live with.

Julia says, My mother bought me Shirley Temple glasses to drink out of. When you come over again, you can drink from them too. I love Shirley Temple. She can sing and dance and everything and she has all those curls in her hair, you could do it too Scags.

I don't want to look like dumb old Shirley Temple, I say and wait for Edna to tell me to be quiet but I guess since we are the only ones here we can talk as loud as we want to. I say out loud, because I'm thinking it and it just comes out—Fuck Shirley Temple. Edna says, Scags none of that. You hear me? I say, Okay. I'm sorry.

I want to read a real story. I want to read about Abraham Lincoln or Beethoven or Clara Barton—Julia says, But Scags you've read all of those. Why are you so angry? Can't you be nice?

Well, I say, yes . . . I can be nice . . . Lets leave and go sing songs, I want to hear you sing your camp songs.

What is that you're talking about? Edna asks and she stands up from behind her table and walks toward us. You know, she says, sometimes you think you want to read but what you really want to is to run around and scream and yell. Maybe today you can't sit quietly in here and look at books.

I look at her mouth moving, her tongue and lips all move. I see the pencil stain on her lower lip and when I look at her eyes, I see how pretty she is.

I say, We'll leave now, come on Julia.

But Julia doesn't want to leave right away. I say, We can come back in a little while. Edna takes the book Julia is looking at, an illustrated dictionary with big pictures of bicycles in there but no pictures of the tandem bike she got as a present. Julia stomps out of the bookmobile, stomps to her front lawn and lies down on the grass on her back and looks at the sky. She is angry at me.

Mrs. Showalter is going to be my teacher, she says.

Oh shit, I say. Well hell's bells, I continue and put my hand over my mouth so that I don't say anymore what is on my mind. I say to Julia with my hand over my mouth, Me too.

What? Julia says. I can't understand you. Are you in my class?

I shake my head back and forth, up and down, from side to side.

Well what is it Scags?

I take my hand down. I take a deep breath and will only say, Me too. I don't want to be angry at Julia. I don't want to hate her but I do, so I say bye to her. She raises a hand to me so I can help her off the ground

but I walk away. When she calls out Scags, want to go
for a bike ride, I just keep walking to my house.

Bowling II

It is Saturday night, no Odessa, just the three of us and after dinner Pops says, Let's go bowling. Mama sits up straight in her chair before I can say, Yeah, let's go, let's go tonight, right now. Let's get out of this house and go somewhere where there are more interesting things to do, let's let's. Mama says before I can say that, How many beers have you had Nate? I don't care how many beers he's had, he can still bowl and I'll get one of those little balls, the lightweight ones and Pops will help me roll it down the lane.

Mama says, We'll go for a line, that's all. Pops says, What's the rush? Scags can come too, which of course I had already planned, the thought had never entered my mind that they would leave me behind.

We go to the bowling alley and it is full of the smack and clatter and rumble of big black balls traveling very fast down the alley and knocking over lots of pins. I stand on a seat and watch everyone, see that funny walk to the line, the arm stretched out, a ball rolling,

rolling, will it knock those white pins down?

Pops gets the lane and the shoes and the balls, Mama goes with him. I go to our lane and sit down waiting. I see a boy from my school with his parents, a silly boy I really don't know, he leaves his parents and runs to me. He has a funny grin on his face when he comes over and says, What happened to your hair? I reach for my head as if something had happened, but of course, it is just my new short style and I say, Do you like it? Ronnie shakes his head yes and I say, Good, I did it for your. He giggles and runs back to his parents. I wait for Pops.

He has a pair of shoes for me and when I put my feet in them they feel hard and uncomfortable as if they were made out of wood. We go looking for a ball. Mama picks one for herself and says, This'll do, but Pops tells Mama it's too heavy, pick a lighter ball. Pops loves to bowl. Pops loves to make the pins fly and he whistles the opening to Beethoven's Fifth Symphony because it sounds like the collision of ball and pins.

He picks a really light ball for me. He tells me to put my fingers in the holes and hang onto the ball. It fits. It's just right and I run in my shoes to where Mama sits tying up her shoes that look funny on her feet, make them look bigger and thinner. Pops goes up first and takes a practice ball. I have perfect form, he tells me. He takes those funny steps and crosses over himself and the ball flies in the air and lands halfway down with a shudder like thunder and the pins all go down.

Perfect, he says. Mama goes next. Pops goes to get a beer. He turns to her and asks if she'd like a beer but she makes a face at him and starts to say something and then he's gone.

Mama takes a practice shot. It rolls fast and hard on the wooden floor and then the pins explode as she hits that magic spot where the pins have no choice but to all fall down. Then it's my turn and I want to wait for Pops but Mama says she'll help me so we walk together down the line. I roll my ball, which naturally goes in the gutter and wiggles slowly all the way down. Oh Scags, she says, touches my cheek. She hasn't done that in a long time.

Pops returns with two bottles of beer. Mama says, I told you I didn't want one. They're for me, he says and sets them in the little holes in the desk where he starts scoring, writing our names on the scoresheet as if we were really good at this.

Pops says, Scags you're first. Go pick up your ball and aim for the sweet spot. I hold the ball up to my nose and see the point the curve makes and take big steps, big steps, and get to the line, let go of the ball and I do this over and over. When it is my turn and every now and then I knock over five or six pins. Mama bowls about as good as Pops. He tells her to join a bowling league. He says, Bev, you could join a league and really improve your game. I don't want you to think, Pops says, that you're not good now, but it would be a little exercise and socializing simultaneously, a night with the ladies—Nate, Mama says, just bowl, will you?

Pops gets up and I see him hold onto the chair for a moment and then he's steady, gets his big black ball, holds his hand over the fan that dries it and he does his perfect motion. He gets a strike. Pops stands staring at the downed pins. He doesn't move until Mama says, Nate, you got a strike. How do I score this? He walks away from us toward the bar and gets another beer.

We play three lines. My fingers are all black and sticky. Mama gets better and better. Pops shows her how to keep score and I wait my turn to bowl but I think I am too little for this game. Maybe if Pops showed me better what to do or even Mama. Well, she did, but she doesn't know the finer points of the game, Pops says, as he swallows down another cold beer. Mama and I try hard. Pops doesn't seems to have to try. Sometimes after he gets a strike he yells too loud and then he misses all the pins for two or three tries. Then he gets angry.

When we finish the third line, Mama says, That's enough. I'm glad. We take off our bowling shoes and Pops has trouble counting the money to pay for everything. Mama tells Pops he has to give her the car keys. When we go to the car, Pops gets in back with me and puts his head in my lap. It is heavy and sweaty. I smell beer. I don't like it.

Pops is quiet as Mama drives out of the parking lot. Maybe he's asleep I think and run my finger down his nose. He catches my finger and holds onto it. Pops says to Mama, You know we could have had some fun if you'd loosened up a bit. You know we could go dancing every night if you were more romantic. We could have another child, if you weren't so afraid of me.

Nate, Mama says, this is not a good time to go into all of that. Well, when would be a good time? We could talk later, Mama says. Pops says, You know you're not the only woman who finds me attractive. Plenty of women would like to be with me. Why only yesterday I was in Boomer's apartment and the cleaning woman said, Oh, Mr. Morgenstern, you're such a nice man, won't you be the father of my child? One of the secretaries in the building where I work, going up in the elevator, she practically got down on the floor for me—Nate, Mama says, I told you this isn't a good time.

He raises himself off my lap and hangs over the seat. He starts punching Mama hard in the arm until she says, Stop it Nate. What do you think you're doing? I say, Stop, stop, stop to both of them. Pops turns to me as if he didn't know I was in the car, as if he hadn't been resting his head in my lap. He sits back. Mama pulls our car into the driveway. Pops puts his hands over his head. He says, I don't know what's happening to me. Mama is crying. I can hear her. She looks in the rearview mirror at Pops. I wish Pops would just be himself again, and put me on his lap, take me for a ride at night, let the wind come racing through the window and we'd be laughing and singing. We would drive so fast and I would learn how to drive in the dark.

43

The Empty House

I'm going to get Davy, I say to Odessa as she tucks my pillow under the green summer spread, light green, a color I don't have in my crayons. I say, He's got to meet Julia. Do you think he'll like Julia like he likes me? Well, I don't want him to like Julia as much but couldn't we all be friends?

Odessa says, Three's a bad number. I don't know why you want to play with that boy.

What do you mean? I ask Odessa. She stands up straight, puts her hands on her hips and says, Look here Scags, I know you like Davy and all that but when you get a little older you'll see, these Mama's boys don't get up to anything good. I don't think you should play with him now that Julia's home. But I like Davy, too, I say. Even with that eye? Odessa says, and then says, Ah, funny face, you don't know who your real friends are, do you? I look at Odessa bend down and pat the pillow and stand up. What makes you say Davy is not my friend? I ask her.

Because he has a look in his eyes that says, I-love-you-so-bleed-for-me look. I know that look. Oh Odessa, Davy is my friend, I say. Go play with Davy then but don't bring anymore snails in here and no more jars of bugs on the patio.

But Odessa, I say, but she plugs in the vacuum cleaner and turns it on. She isn't able to talk to me anymore, so I run downstairs, out the front door and jump off the front stoop. Should I get my bike? Should I have gotten my holster so Davy and I can play cowboys and Indians? I run across the front lawn, into the open garage where Mama's car sits like a white rabbit ready to jump out of its hole. I pull my bike out of its spot between Mama's car and the cinder block wall of the garage.

I climb on my bike and ride down the driveway with my feet off the pedals and I go so fast I miss the turn and slam into a tree. Down I go with a clatter of metal on cement, my knee on the sidewalk. I turn back to the house to see if anyone saw what happened. No one. So why cry, I say, and pick up the bike and brush the dirt off my knee. My elbow is bleeding and so what, I say, and get back on the bike and ride down the street, around the corner, past where Julia lives. Her house is all open. The breezes run right through it making everything smell of fresh cut flowers, watermelon and ice cream. I don't see Julia in her back yard so I keep going to Davy's house.

When I get to his front walk, I put my kickstand

down and spit on both my hands, rub them together, then spit into them again and rub my elbow and knee. Elbow and knee ole, I say. On the door there is a big chain and a lock. I knock on the door. No noise inside. I try the bell and I hear the gong go through the house but no footsteps coming to let me in. Well, I say, who could open the door with this look on it? I jump off the steps and run to the window. The drapes are open and I see all their furniture, all of it, even Davy's red wagon.

I put both hands on the window and fit my face between them. Maybe there is some clue I could see as to where he is. When did he leave? Why didn't he say anything? Are they on a trip?

I hear a voice, it's the mailman. Looks like they had to get out in a hurry, he says. I've got more bills for them which they won't be paying. He holds up a stack of letters so I can see them. More mail than we get, I say to him. I know, he says, where'd they go to? We both stand there not knowing how we could have missed them leaving and now we don't know where they are. Why is there a lock on the door, I ask him. He says, Probably couldn't afford this big house.

The mailman walks away, towards Julia's house. I run around the house twice to see if there are any clues. The dust and sand in their yard gets all over my shoes and what is Odessa going to say when she sees this mess?

I leave Davy's yard, get back on my bike and start

to ride around the block the long way and maybe I can figure out where he went. I push the pedals down and around and reach the next corner before I want to. I slow down now because I don't want to fall off the bike again.

I know Davy will come back and the three of us can play together. I still have Julia. I'll pretend I'm in a race between me and the Lone Ranger to get to Tonto who has fallen into quicksand and whoever gets there first will be able to save him. I race past the Mills' house, past the new house that isn't finished yet, and then a ways down the street, I pass the Cooks' house. There is Mama looking for me. I start to cry, I cry so hard my bike wobbles and I jump off it and let it crash to the ground. I hear its banged up crash and run as fast as I can to Mama, holding my elbow then my knee, my elbow and my knee. I run to Mama and bury my head in her and wrap myself around her.

Mama takes my arms from around her and lifts my face up to hers. She says, What's wrong? How did you get hurt like that? I can't talk and I can't stop crying. I sob and snort and mucus is coming out of my nose and my throat aches as if I had a strep throat and my elbow and knee really hurt. Mama pulls me away from her and takes a look. She pushes the hair off my forehead and the sweat cools at her touch.

Mama says, Let's go inside. She takes my hand and I walk beside her, I'm so glued to her leg that if she doesn't hurry up inside I'm going to melt into her. We get inside and Mama calls Odessa who comes from the basement and Mama tells her to clean me up.

It's not that I can't clean myself. It's that it hurts. It's not that Mama can't do it, but that she thinks Odessa can do it too and she says she has an appointment now. I let go of Mama and rub my eyes. Odessa says, Keep those filthy hands away from your face, Scags. I stop crying.

Mama leaves. I yell to her, Where are you going? Mama says, I'll be back in a little while and I'll bring your bike in. After Odessa gets you set, you go lie down for a while. You'll see. It was just a nasty fall. You'll be fine.

I watch Mama walk away as she is talking. Out she goes and Odessa takes my hand and leads me into the kitchen. She keeps bandaids and stuff there for her burns and scratches when she's cooking. I hear Mama's car door slam. The engine starts. The car backs out. The garage door goes down.

Odessa washes me and hums, Lady Be Good, and if I start to cry again it won't be too good. Bactine. Bandaid. A pat on my butt and I go up to my room. Odessa walks with me. I say, Davy's gone.

White And Red

Pops is going to work tomorrow. Today is Sunday so tonight Mama will cook dinner. That means I had better stock up on some candy. I leave my room and listen outside Mama and Pops' room. Quiet. They must still be sleeping. I go downstairs and take my bike out of the garage and ride to the drug store and buy a Three Musketeers because I only have fifty cents and I want to save some for ice cream after dinner.

On the ride back, the air feels very wet and like some wooly thing has jumped in a pool and fallen on top of me. It's hard to breathe and as I pass Witch's Well I ride fast because even though it's not night it gives me the creeps. I hear a siren coming behind me. I turn around. An ambulance with a police car behind it. They go past me so fast that all the dirt in the street attacks my face.

I try to ride as fast as the ambulance, but only get as far as the school yard before I am too tired to ride fast anymore. Where did they go? It takes all my energy to catch my breath and to forget about riding like an angel through the streets. I have no wings and I have no magic powers and the sirens are long gone.

I see Ricky Rappaport playing at the basketball court in back of the school all by himself. Hey Ricky, I say, where is everyone? I ride over to him and he says, They're coming soon enough, want to play horse? I watch as he dribbles and makes a lay up. I say, No, not today, I'm going home. See ya.

I ride the rest of the blocks to my house and I really want to eat my candy bar but when I get to the corner I see the ambulance and police car in front of my house. Their lights are flashing and they make me scared because Mama is standing on the front lawn in her bathrobe. When she turns to me I see it is covered with big red spots, dark ones, purple, all of it blood.

I throw my bike down, run to her and see she is crying and that her new hairdo is all messed up. Mrs. Arthur puts out her arm to me to hold me. Where have you been? Mama asks. I say, No where, I just went for a ride. I keep wanting to touch her but Mrs. Arthur holds me back. Is it because she's all bloody or maybe she's angry at me?

Where's Pops? I say, where's Pops. She says, Oh your Pops did it this time. She takes my hand and tells me to be quiet now. A stretcher comes out of the garage. They have Pops on it and he's not awake. They run the stretcher down the driveway into the back of the ambulance. The men lift it up and shove it in as if they

were closing a drawer. Mama tells me to wait for her
and she runs inside and then quickly comes out with
her purse and locks the house, we get in her car and
follow the ambulance and police car to the hospital.

I don't know what to say and Mama sits behind
the wheels gritting her teeth. I feel tears running on
my cheeks and wipe them away with the back of my
hand which feels hot and I don't have a thought in my
head, it's as if we, Mama and me, were taking a drive
to the dentist rather than to the hospital following
an ambulance with Pops lying in the back of it not
knowing where we are.

What happened Mama, what happened? Mama holds
tight to the steering wheel. She looks straight ahead.
I don't know how far we have to go but I just want to
sit in the car forever, until I'm grown up.

Mama says, Scags, your Pops tried to kill himself.
Why? I ask, why? Mama says, I don't know. But you'll
see, they'll fix him up really good and then we will
bring him home. I hold myself to myself and I am so
cold. I could use a blanket. I could use a chance to be
with some angel now telling me Mama's right.

In the hospital, they wheel Pops behind a heavy door.
I wait on one of the benches while Mama goes in with
him. I wait and wait. A little baby, crying, is carried
in with its Mama and they go to a desk where a tired
woman sits in a green uniform. A doctor comes out and
takes the baby and mother into another room.

I'm left alone. The policeman comes over to me and

sits down while he writes something in his book. I'm thirsty but I can't reach the drinking fountain, I say to him. He looks at me and says, That your father we picked up on Kolmar? I say, Yes, what happened to him? We walk to the drinking fountain and he picks me up so I can get a drink. The water is so cold I get a headache. He puts me down. He says, Your father tried to do himself in. But your mother caught him just in time. You're a lucky kid. He walks away from me, over to the doors and goes in. I'm a lucky kid I say over and over. I'm a lucky kid.

I want my Mama but she is in with Pops so long and when she finally comes out she is crying. She talks to the policeman who looks at her very nicely. They talk in low whispers. I want to hear what they are saying. But I know they'll stop talking if I go over there.

I go to the window instead and look out at the woods. I start whistling When the Saints Go Marching In.

Well You Know

Mama, Mrs. Arthur and I are sitting in the kitchen where the two of them are smoking and drinking cups of black coffee. Mama stubs out her cigarette and goes upstairs to her bedroom to change out of her robe. Mrs. Arthur sits with me. I say, Mrs. Arthur, Mrs. Arthur—I can't think of anything else to say to her. She pats my hand and says, It's okay. Mama comes back downstairs in a pair of shorts and wearing one of Pops' old blue shirts. She kneels in front of me, her hands resting on my knees and those hands are cold. Mama says, You do know your Pops is going to be okay? We have to be very patient until he comes back to us and we have to be good, very good so that he will have a wonderful family to come back to.

Mama, I say, the house smells bad. Yes, Mama says, your father made quite a mess that I've got to clean up this morning.

Mrs. Arthur says, I'll help you Bev. Mama says, No Ginger, it's nice of you to offer, but he made such a mess of that bathroom that I can't let anyone see what he has done.

Scags, Mama says, and stands up, go outside and play, go outside for a while. I'm sure you'll be fine now, right? Mama starts to cry. Mrs. Arthur tells me to go out now, that she'll look after Mama and help her clean up and then the house will smell fresh and that Pops will be able to come home soon.

I get off my chair and take a peek around the corner but his bathroom door is closed, broken, but closed. I go out the back door, leaving the two of them behind me. I sneak under the window and listen. I hear Mama crying. Mrs. Arthur tells her, it's okay, go ahead and cry and then Mama starts talking in a loud voice as if Mrs. Arthur was a far ways away. Mama says, He slashed himself with a razor all up his neck and wrists. I don't know where I got the strength to break down that door—

I don't want to listen anymore. I go out further in the yard, under my tree. I lie on my back and I feel myself falling, falling, falling, and I don't know where I will land, but it's scary. My arms, legs and head are falling into different places, each one having its own hole to fall into. Two legs. Two arms. One head. All cut off me. All rolling down a hill. Falling into the earth, collapsed. I can tell they are trying not to fall asleep because that is even scarier. I can't stop my eyes from closing. I can't tell my mind to stay awake. Yes. I sleep.

When I wake up the sun has moved to the back of the house. The house is still. Quiet. I wonder if I can go in now. I get up and walk to the center of the yard and lie down again. I feel the sun on me. I close my eyes that just do not want to see anything. All I see is gold spots, more and more gold spots jumping. Oh my Pops I love him so , , , Oh please Pops come back and be like you were. I'll never be like I was.

I stay outside listening, smelling the air which is prickly in my nose. I listen to the cicadas making a whirring sound in the cottonwood. I watch the clouds, the big gray clouds come scraping themselves across the blue sky. Something licks my knee, then something licks my fingertips. I think, oh my . . . and then whatever fly buzzed by made me think of a puppy. And that is just how it goes, one thing reminding me of something else until it is time to go inside.